Gold Poison

Caleb Black, ordained minister and bounty hunter, witnesses an attempted bank robbery and, although the two ringleaders escape, Caleb knows who they are and gives chase. He locates them in the gold rush town of Gold Poison but his attempts to arrest the two are foiled by the arrival of a US marshal and his deputies. Marshal Sam Warlock, unlike most other marshals, earns his money by collecting bounty on wanted outlaws.

Forced to hide and protect the two men from falling into the marshal's hands until they reach Morgan City, Caleb finds himself pitted against the combined might of the marshal and his deputies. Can Caleb prevail and collect the bounty himself?

ROYAL BOROUGH OF GREENWICH

Follow us on twitter @greenwichlibs

Mobile and Home Service at Plumstead Library
Plumstead High Street, SE18 1JL
020 8319 5875

Please return by the last date shown

10/16 MANDELA 0 3 DEC 2016 2 9 DEC 2016 →MO 21/7 Murray →OU 6/17 Murray -- JUN 2017 LEO COLEMAN MAR 2018 MINNIE BENNETT OCT 2019 GARNER CHASE -- DEC 2019	BILL -- MAR 2020 WIDER CAT -- SEP 2021 Mandela -- AUG 2023 COLLERSTON USE -- JAN 2024 BILL WALDEN -- JUL 2024 ROSE -- SEP 2024	

Thank you! To renew, please contact any
Royal Greenwich library or renew online at
www.better.org.uk/greenwichlibraries

Gold Poison

L. D. TETLOW

A Black Horse Western

ROBERT HALE · LONDON

Typeset by
Derek Doyle & Associates, Liverpool.
Printed and bound in Great Britain by
Antony Rowe Limited, Wiltshire.

ONE

He had recognized two of the seven men now leaning on the bar counter. Three of the seven were black men, three plainly white despite the ingrained grime on their faces and one who appeared to be a half-caste Indian. The two whom he recognized - from wanted posters he had in his saddlebag - were Billy McGovern, a white man and Leroy Smith, a black man. Smith might have been his correct name, although Caleb very much doubted it, but it did not matter.

As far as Caleb was concerned, the colour of the men's skin was of no significance whatsoever, although he was well aware from personal experience that in some places and to some people such things did matter. All he was concerned with was that as wanted outlaws McGovern was worth $1,500 and Smith another $1,000. He had little doubt that the other five men also had prices on their heads and would probably increase the value of the gang considerably.

There was no doubt about it, he was looking at some extremely valuable property, valuable enough to enable many men to retire should they be lucky enough to collect the rewards. Possible retirement though, was not on Caleb's mind at that moment.

The Reverend Caleb Black – black by name and black by his skin colour – in addition to being an ordained minister of religion, made the greater part of his living as a bounty hunter. From time to time he would be called upon to perform various pastoral duties and in most cases he was only too happy to oblige. In fact he quite enjoyed that side of his life occasionally. He did not think for one moment that any of the seven men would be calling upon him for such duties. As far as he was concerned their souls were beyond redemption but their value as outlaws most certainly was not.

Had there been only one, or perhaps even two of them, he would have had no hesitation in taking them to the nearest sheriff there and then. However, seven violent outlaws represented odds against him which were certainly not in his favour. Even considering the possible rewards, Caleb was not foolish enough to believe he could tackle seven of them at once. He also suspected that this fact had some great influence as to why they were still at large.

The vast majority of small town sheriffs, like Caleb, were not prepared to tackle that many men at once. In fact some would not even tackle a lone outlaw. Caleb had long since learned that dealing with drunks and the occasional bar brawl were the limits of most sheriffs' capabilities or even ambitions.

The small town of Burney did have a sheriff, Caleb had seen him slouched in a wicker chair sunning himself outside his office a few minutes before he had entered the saloon. He had also seen the seven men ride into town and go into the saloon, which was when he thought he recognized at least two of them. He knew for definite that the sheriff had seen them as well. He had confirmed that McGovern and Smith were wanted outlaws by checking his many posters but he could not identify the others. His visit to the saloon was mainly to double check on them.

The men casually glanced at him as he too leaned against the counter and ordered a beer – which proved surprisingly good, which was unusual. There was no significance in another black face – Caleb had seen at least five other such faces in town – and the men ignored him. In fact they appeared to be in deep conversation and were even arguing amongst themselves.

Caleb pretended uninterest, drank his beer and wandered out into the street. He looked up and down, noting the various stores and other businesses. He was curious because he knew from experience that men like McGovern and Smith looked at every town as a potential for robbery, although even they sometimes ignored small stores since it was very unlikely that any store would provide sufficient money to satisfy all seven of them. Store robberies were usually carried out by lone outlaws in desperate need of cash.

Burney had all the usual stores associated with a farming community; a general store, a hardware store, a butcher, a gunsmith, a baker, a bootmaker, a barber who also advertised hot baths, and a ladies' milliner and haberdashery. There was also a livery-stable-cum-blacksmith and a corn- and seed-merchant down one of the side streets and a church at the far end of the town. He did not believe that any of these, the gunsmith possibly excepted, would be of interest to the seven men now in deep conversation in the saloon. If they were planning anything, and Caleb felt that they could well be doing so, it would have to be something rather more important.

There was one building which most such outlaws – particularly those with a previous history of such robberies – could well find irresistible. This was a bank, quite a large bank if size of building was anything to go by. Both McGovern and Smith had a previous history of bank robbery. In fact McGovern was also wanted for the murder of a bank clerk.

Caleb wandered across to the sheriff, who was still lounging outside his office. The sheriff did not even move as Caleb stood in front of him. Not only did he not move, his eyes remained stubbornly shut. Caleb waited a few moments, knowing that the sheriff was fully aware of his presence.

'Want somethin', boy?' the sheriff eventually drawled without opening his eyes. 'Cain't you see I'm havin' my siesta?'

Caleb smiled to himself. The sheriff was plainly from one of the more southerly states.

'I just thought you'd like to know you've got seven outlaws in town,' said Caleb.

'I know, I seen 'em,' the sheriff drawled again. 'Could be I got me eight outlaws. I seen you ride in too.'

'No, only seven,' said Caleb. 'I know who two of them are. One of the white men is Billy McGovern and one of the black men is Leroy Smith. Both have large rewards out on their heads.'

'An' how come you know so much, boy,' sneered the sheriff, this time opening his eyes.

'Because I'm a bounty hunter,' said Caleb. 'It's my business to know about such things.'

'Bounty hunter, eh?' said the sheriff. If he was at all surprised he certainly did not show it. 'I ain't never seen me a black bounty hunter before.' He looked Caleb up and down and smirked again. 'No, sir, never even knew such an animal existed. Now if'n you hadn't told me you was a bounty hunter, I would have sworn you was some kind of preacher. I seen plenty of black preachers before. You sure dress like a preacher but that gun on your hip sure tells me different. I ain't never seen a preacher sportin' a gun before.'

'The Reverend Caleb Black,' said Caleb by way of introduction. 'I *am* an ordained minsiter, but I decided many years ago that saving the souls of outlaws and collecting the bounty out on them was far more profitable than just praying for men's souls. Did you know you had seven outlaws in town?'

'I guessed they were,' said the sheriff. 'I ain't actually got round to checkin' on who they are though. Plenty of time for that. Seems like there's no need, you appear to have all the answers.'

'I only know two of them,' said Caleb. 'There's a total of two thousand five hundred dollars out on just those two. . . .' For a second or two the sheriff's eyes showed some interest. Just his eyes, not his face. 'I'd like to stake my claim on that reward money here and now.'

'You just hand 'em over, boy,' sneered the sheriff,

'an' I'll gladly see to the rest of it.'

'One man against seven?' queried Caleb. 'I might be good, Sheriff, but I'm not that good. I'm going to need some help.'

'That's what I like to see, a modest black preacher,' the sheriff drawled. 'Help don't come cheap, boy, what had you in mind? You got all the aces, you can collect the reward, I cain't. Most law men ain't allowed to collect. Maybe I should be a bounty hunter too. Thought about it a couple of times but I reckon it's too much like hard work an' too dangerous.'

'It has its good and bad times but I manage,' said Caleb. 'How does half of the reward money sound?'

'That sounds fair enough,' said the sheriff, for the first time showing some real interest. 'For a bounty hunter you don't seem all that bad. Most wouldn't share the pickin's from their nose. Come on inside, boy. I'd say it was time we checked on just who they are. Far as I'm concerned you got yourself a deal.'

'Just one thing, Sheriff,' said Caleb. 'I'm not your *boy*. I am not a slave and never have been and I am most certainly not related to you in any way. I was also a lieutenant on the Union side during the war.'

'Lieutenant, eh? It figures, them Yankees was never too particular who they made officers.' The sheriff grinned. 'Take no heed of me, that's just my way. I guess all that makes you somethin' of a different kind of black man in your eyes, but you're all the same as far as I'm concerned. There's good blacks an' there's bad blacks. I ain't figured out which you are an' I don't really care. You probably worked out I ain't from these parts by my accent. I hail from Texas originally. Came this way on account of my wife was from round here. Callin' you *boy* is just my way, it don't mean nothin'.'

'Understood, Sheriff,' said Caleb. 'Right now I suppose it doesn't matter what you call me, there's a lot of money at stake.'

The sheriff simply grinned and pulled a sheaf of wanted posters from a drawer which he placed in front of Caleb. They both thumbed through the posters and, in addition to the posters of Billy McGovern and Leroy Smith, Caleb picked out three more which probably were of three of the men. The one almost certainly was, the half-breed Indian.

'Jimmy Two Rivers,' said Caleb, pushing the poster in front of the sheriff. 'Bank robbery, stagecoach hold-up and various stores. Suspected of murder but no definite proof. I'd say that was him all right. These other two could be the other two white men, but I can't be absolutely certain. I can't see any that look like the other two black men. I'll bet there's flyers out on them somewhere though.'

'Sure to be,' agreed the sheriff. 'I got me some more here, take a look through 'em. You reckon they're plannin' a robbery right here in Burney?'

'I don't *know* anything, Sheriff,' said Caleb. 'But there was something about the way they were acting which makes me think they might be. I'd say Burney was an ideal place for them to try just that.' He was examining the new posters and continued: 'Remote town, fairly wealthy from the look of it. One sheriff, decent sized bank. Yes, Sheriff, I'd say it is quite possible.'

'Sure, you could be right,' conceded the sheriff. 'So

what do you plan on doin'? We could take 'em before they get a chance or we could wait for them to try somethin'. Right now is the hottest part of the day, most folk'll be havin' their siesta. You would too if'n you had any sense, but I guess outlaws intent on robbin' a bank, a bounty huntin' black preacher an' bank employees don't take siestas. OK, boy, I'm with you. I need the money just as much as you.'

'Two against seven,' said Caleb. 'At least that's better odds than one against seven, but it still leaves them with the advantage. They probably know most folk will be asleep so it's a perfect time to rob the bank. How many men with guns can you raise?'

'Like I say, bank don't have no afternoon siesta,' said the sheriff. 'I reckon I could find three, maybe four men with guns if I had to. Only trouble with involvin' more men though is that they'll all want a share of any reward. I'm all for a half-share but I ain't so sure about any less.' He looked Caleb up and down and smiled. 'I see you're a two-gun man. That's unusual in itself but a two-gun-totin' black, bounty huntin' preacher must be a first. Can you use both guns?'

'There's been a good many outlaws who have discovered too late that I can,' said Caleb. 'I must admit that I tend to agree with you that the fewer there are to share the reward with the better. Besides, most sharing deals usually lead to arguments about who did what and who deserves more. Do you think we can take all seven between the two of us?'

'Won't know until we try, boy,' drawled the sheriff. 'Worst thing that can happen is we both get killed, in which case money won't be much use to us.'

'I admire your confidence,' sneered Caleb. 'I for one certainly don't intend to get killed. I might be a man of God but I'm not quite ready to meet my maker.'

Caleb found two more posters which could well have been the two remaining black men, although each had rewards of only $100. He made a quick mental calculation.

$2,500 for McGovern and Smith, $500 for a white man apparently called James Bennett, $300 for the other white man called Ernie Wells, $100 for each of the other two black men and a surprising $1,000 for the half-breed.

'I make that four thousand five hundred dollars in total,' said Caleb. 'Not a bad day's work if you can get it.'

'Two thousand two hundred an' fifty apiece,' mused the sheriff. 'I reckon I'll be able to give up this job on that kind of money. Can't think of any other way to get my hands on that much.'

'And do what, Sheriff?' asked Caleb. 'There doesn't seem to be that much to do round here.'

'Go back to Texas I reckon,' said the sheriff. 'Ain't nothin' to keep me round here now. My wife died last year an' my two kids have long since gone. I got some family back in Texas. My boy's an officer in the army. Captain he is now. Only thing is he's in the wrong army, but then there ain't no Confederate Army no more. My daughter married and went off to California.'

'First we have to get those outlaws,' said Caleb, who had been looking out of the window. 'It would appear that they're about to move. They've just come out of the saloon.' The sheriff joined him. 'Did you say the bank doesn't close for a siesta?' continued Caleb.

'No, never has done, even though hardly anyone ever uses it at this time of day,' confirmed the sheriff.

'And from the way those men are acting I'd say they know it too,' said Caleb. 'Look, they're splitting up. McGovern and Smith are heading for the bank, two across here and the other three round the back towards the bank. It's time we moved, Sheriff.'

'Back way!' said the sheriff, grabbing a rifle. 'We can get out unseen before they get round the back of the bank. If they're as bad as they're supposed to be we'd probably be shot the moment we went out on to the street if we went out the front way, especially with guns.'

Caleb agreed and both slipped quietly out of the back door. The sheriff indicated that Caleb should go to the left while he went to the right in the direction of the rear of the bank. There was no time for Caleb to argue and he slipped along a narrow alleyway, gun at the ready.

He peered round the corner of the building and saw the two black men who had crossed the street standing outside the sheriff's office, although neither appeared to have tried the door to the office. It was plainly their job to deal with the sheriff should he show his face.

Caleb decided that he could probably get close to the men without arousing suspicion. They had seen him before and a man walking along a boardwalk was something quite normal. He returned his gun to his holster and stepped out, making certain that both his guns were well hidden under his coat.

'Good afternoon.' Caleb smiled as he approached them. 'I saw you in the saloon a little earlier. Allow me to introduce myself. I am the Reverend Caleb—'

'Ain't got no time to listen now, Reveren',' said one of the men. 'If you don't want to get yoursel' hurt, I suggest you get the hell out of it right now.'

'Hurt?' asked Caleb with another broad smile. 'Why, is something about to happen? How exciting . . .' Before either man knew what was happening Caleb had drawn both his guns and had pressed one into each man's ribs. 'I do believe it's you who might get hurt,' said Caleb. 'You . . .' He prodded his gun hard into the ribs of the man nearest the office door. 'Open that door and go inside. I think we can accommodate you. Move!'

Both men stared wide-eyed at Caleb but did not attempt to run or go for their guns. The one did as he was told and opened the door. All three went inside where Caleb instructed them to throw their guns on to the floor. At the far end of the room was a single cell with a key already in the lock. Caleb ordered one of them to open the door and he pushed both inside. He grinned broadly as he turned the key in the lock and removed it.

'I'll just go and bring your friends in,' he said.

'What the hell you doin', Reveren'?' demanded one of them. 'We ain't done nothin' an' you ain't got no right to lock us up. You ain't no sheriff.'

'You can complain to the judge or the Good Lord,' said Caleb. He went out of the office, this time by the front door.

He looked along the street and saw McGovern and Smith still outside the bank. They were obviously allow-ing time for the others to get into position. Quite suddenly there were several shouts from behind the

15

bank followed by shooting. Caleb's first thought was for the sheriff and he raced down an alley where he found the sheriff crouching behind a water butt, clutching his shoulder. There appeared to be quite a lot of blood.

'Bastards saw me,' he hissed. 'I got one of 'em though. Other two are holed up behind that pile of wood.'

'Hold them there,' instructed Caleb. 'I'm going to get McGovern and Smith.'

He raced back along the alley, expecting the two outlaws to have made an attempt on the bank, but he was wrong. He arrived just in time to see both men riding away as fast as they could. For a brief moment Caleb considered using one of the other horses and going after them, but a volley of shots from the rear of the building made him change his mind. He ran past the bank and down another alley which brought him behind the men taking cover behind the wood. They saw him but not in time. Two quick shots soon dispatched them.

The wound to the sheriff's shoulder was little more than a flesh wound, although it bled profusely. Caleb ripped a piece off the sheriff's shirt and told the sheriff to hold it on the wound. By that time several of the good citizens of Burney had arrived.

'Get a doctor,' Caleb ordered. 'Your sheriff's been hurt.' One man dashed off.

The sheriff assured Caleb that he was fine and Caleb went to examine the three outlaws who had been shot. Two of them, the white men James Bennett and Ernie Wells, were dead. The half-breed, Jimmy Two Rivers was still alive but had a large, bloody wound in his chest.

The doctor arrived and, at Caleb's insistence, dealt with the sheriff first. He then examined the other three, agreed that the two white men were dead and stated that in his opinion there was little he could do for the Indian. In fact Jimmy Two Rivers died as he was being moved to the sheriff's office.

The sheriff showed some surprise when he saw the two black men locked in the cell, but he did not comment. His wound was dressed properly by the doctor, then the undertaker – who also traded as a carpenter and timber merchant – was called in to remove the bodies.

'McGovern and Smith managed to get away,' said Caleb, almost apologetically. 'I suppose that means there isn't quite so much to share. Two thousand dollars, a thousand each. Still, that's better than nothing.'

'Pity,' said the sheriff. 'Still, like you say, boy, a thousand dollars is better'n nothin' an' a hell of a lot more'n I could ever hope to save from what I earn. Maybe I'll still head back to Texas. I've got me a couple of hundred stashed away so I won't be too badly off. All we got to do now is file for the reward. We're in luck, the circuit judge is due here in two days, he can sign the authorization.'

'Two days,' mused Caleb. 'I was hoping to go after McGovern and Smith.'

'You're a bounty hunter,' the sheriff pointed out. 'You must know the system. In small towns like this we can't just hand over the money without an order from a judge. We could send a wire to Maryville but that'll still take a couple of days an' they could be awkward.

Might as well wait for the judge. Don't worry about McGovern an' Smith, they'll still be there. Men like that don't like the open country, they don't go too far from towns. They like to spend their money on drink, gamblin' an' women.'

'I suppose they do,' sighed Caleb. 'OK. In the meantime though I claim their horses, saddles and guns as mine. That's normal practice. It helps boost reward money on most outlaws. You'd be surprised at just how little money there is on some of them. I've regularly had to settle for fifty dollars.'

'Go ahead,' agreed the sheriff. 'Just remember, though, I expect half-share of anythin' you get.'

Caleb collected the outlaws' guns, five revolvers, five rifles, one of which appeared to be an almost new Winchester, five saddles and five horses. There were other things such as bedrolls and cooking-pots, but he was unable to sell these. The two men in the jail had eight dollars and a few cents between them and the other three had a total of forty-two dollars and a few cents, all of which Caleb took and put in his pocket.

It took a certain amount of haggling with both blacksmith and gunsmith, which was quite normal, but Caleb eventually added another $350, making a total of $400. After some further consideration, he decided to give this entire amount to the sheriff. He had his sights set on a far larger amount, the $2,500 reward for McGovern and Smith. Having caught scent of that much money, Caleb was in no mood to give up. Once in pursuit, he rarely did.

It seemed that Burney had not had as much excitement in many a year and people suddenly appeared from nowhere simply to stand and gaze at this new phenomenon. For the next few hours he was followed constantly by wide-eyed, wonderous children. He did his best to ignore them – it was nothing new – and a couple of times he suddenly turned and growled at them. Most ran off amid loud squeals of delight only to return a few minutes later to continue the game. A few of the adults queried whether he really was a minister and most remained unconvinced by his assurance that he was.

Burney did not have a hotel but there was a rooming-house so he had little choice. Normally he avoided rooming-houses, mainly because they were a little too basic for his liking and he liked a bit of privacy. However, this particular rooming-house was better than most and at that moment did not have any other guests. He checked for bedbugs but did not see any and agreed to take a bed.

The woman who owned it, a very large but clean white woman, also offered to provide him with a meal. Since there was no other choice, he accepted and was pleasantly surprised. It was basic – mutton stew – but it was well cooked and tasted good. He willingly parted with the two dollars asked for bed and meal.

TWO

McGovern and Smith had ridden off towards the west so, assuming that the sheriff was right in that most outlaws liked to be close to towns, Caleb spent some time studying what few maps there were, trying to work out which way they would go.

The sheriff assured him that it would be most unlikely that they would turn north since that led into at least a hundred miles of desert which also stretched round to the east of Burney. Of course neither man could be certain they would not go that way since they did not know if the two outlaws were aware of that fact. However, as was often the case, certain assumptions needed to be made and Caleb decided that they would probably continue to head west. It was not often that Caleb made the wrong choice.

Caleb also felt, perhaps with a certain amount of arrogance and disdain for small-town sheriffs, that he knew best. His knowledge of outlaw behaviour was most certainly gained through years of experience. He knew that the chosen route and destination of the outlaws would depend very much on whether they felt or knew they were being followed.

If they felt safe then it was highly likely that they would head for a centre of activity and people. If not, they would probably head for the hills and lie low for a while. He had been prepared to chase after them straightaway but now somewhat reluctantly conceded that the delay would give them a sense of security. They would most likely head for one of the towns.

Burney County consisted of a large, flat, fertile plain, which was why the main business of the area was farming. Burney itself was roughly in the centre of that plain. To the west the plain stretched for about another thirty miles before it met a range of mountains. There was one other small town at the foot of the mountains called Clemson, but, according to the sheriff, it was much smaller than Burney and did not have a regular sheriff of its own – it being part of his jurisdiction – and most certainly it did not have a bank. In fact it only had two stores, a general store, which doubled as a saloon, and a hardware store. He admitted that his visits to Clemson were very infrequent, but then hardly anything ever happened there.

According to the sheriff there was only one way across the mountains from Clemson but once on the other side the trail divided. To the south-west the road led, after about thirty miles, to a town called Ashboro which was centred on cattle ranching. The road to the north-west led eventually to a large town known as Morgan City although it was a journey of at least eighty miles once the mountains had been crossed. This, in the opinion of the sheriff, was the most likely destination of the two outlaws.

Ashboro, according to the sheriff, could be ruled out because it was a cattle town and the cowhands there were notoriously hard men who did not take kindly to black men. Since it seemed that both Smith and McGovern had been in the state for some considerable length of time, he felt that Smith would be well aware of towns which were hostile to his kind and avoid them wherever possible. There was no proof that he would know this, it was just a feeling the sheriff had. Caleb was inclined to agree. In fact Caleb had already decided that Morgan City would be the outlaws, and his destination.

Morgan City was apparently large enough for most strangers, no matter what the colour of their skin, to enter and pass through completely unnoticed and was full of whorehouses, gaming-halls and bars. In fact the sheriff claimed it to be a magnet for every saddletramp, down-and-out, ne'er-do-well, gambler and outlaw there ever was. He maintained that Morgan City was nothing but a den of iniquity and fornication. It was plain that the sheriff was not at all enamoured of Morgan City. He admitted that he had only been there twice in his life and had not enjoyed the experience at all.

The sheriff offered to send a wire to Morgan City warning them of the impending arrival of the outlaws but Caleb strongly objected to this idea. He pointed out that it would probably deprive him of the reward money and that the sheriff there probably had enough to contend with if what the sheriff had said was only half true.

The circuit judge arrived a day earlier than expected and the sheriff lost no time in taking the two captured outlaws up before him. Both proved very co-operative and testified that the dead men were indeed James Bennett, Ernie Wells and Jimmy Two Rivers. They also admitted that the plan had been to rob the bank and that they were wanted elsewhere for robbery.

The judge sentenced each to two years in prison and signed the order releasing the reward money. The following morning Caleb collected the money from the bank.

Caleb met the sheriff in his office where, as promised, he divided the reward money equally between them. He also placed the $400 dollars recovered from the men and the sale of their horses, saddles and guns on the table.

'I thought that since we couldn't collect on the other two,' said Caleb, 'you might as well keep this as well. Four hundred dollars, sorry it isn't more. It'll go some way towards your retirement.'

'Now that sure is civil of you, boy.' The sheriff grinned. 'With what I've got saved I reckon I can go back to Texas, maybe buy myself a small farm or a store. What about you?'

'There's still another two thousand five hundred dollars out there for the taking,' said Caleb. 'I'll find them; it isn't often that much money slips through my fingers. Thanks for your help, Sheriff, I don't think I could have done it without you. Sorry about your shoulder.'

'It'll be fine,' said the sheriff. 'It's me who should be thankin' you, *boy* . . .' He deliberately stressed the word *boy*, more in a friendly way than a derogatory way. 'I gotta admit that if'n it'd been left to me, they'd probably have got away with it.'

Caleb left Burney at dawn the following morning. He was in no great hurry; he doubted very much if McGovern and Smith would ride long and hard. As soon as they realized that they were not being followed, they would relax and from experience Caleb had discovered that outlaws who relaxed often made mistakes.

The supposed thirty miles to the hamlet of Clemson

– for that is all it turned out to be – proved, at least in Caleb's opinion, to be closer to forty miles. He did not reach it until mid-morning of the following day. Enquiries showed that a white man and a black man had passed that way, but they had not stopped. He was assured that the road across the mountains was easy to follow but very steep in parts and so it proved to be.

It took Caleb another two days to cross the mountains, although had he pushed his horse a little harder, he thought he might have been able to make it in one day. As expected, shortly after descending on to flat ground, the trail divided as it crossed a river. There was only one signpost, which indicated that Morgan City was off to the right. It did not state how far the city was.

Early the following morning, after having shot a rabbit and spent the night alongside a fast-flowing river, Caleb came across another and completely unexpected signpost. It was a simple and rather crude sign, but it indicated that somewhere glorying under the name of Gold Poison City lay along that route. He tried to recall the map he had studied but certainly could not remember anywhere with such a strange name.

He thought about which way McGovern and Smith might have elected to go and, for some strange reason, he thought that they would have felt, just as he did, compelled to investigate such a place. He turned off the main trail and headed for Gold Poison City, wondering exactly what he would find when he eventually reached it. It did seem obvious that it had something to do with gold, but then again it was not always the case. Sometimes men gave places very strange names for some very strange reasons. The sign had given no indication as to how far it was to Gold Poison.

It was mid-afternoon when Caleb saw two men riding mules and heading towards him. The men, both bearded, were plainly prospectors. He had seen such men many times. At first they were very wary of Caleb and even drew a gun on him as they approached. It was plainly a very ancient gun but it could still be lethal. Caleb smiled and raised his hands. This one act told him that the prospectors were probably carrying either gold or lots of money.

'Good day to you, gentlemen,' he greeted. 'Please, put that gun away, they do have a nasty habit of going off and killing people.'

'Now that's mighty fancy talk, 'specially from the likes of you,' said the one. 'Yep, guns do have a habit of goin' off, that's what they're supposed to do.'

He did put the gun away and Caleb breathed a little easier. Had it been necessary he had no doubt that he could have dealt with the men, especially since they appeared to have only the one ancient pistol between them. But he was not looking for trouble, at least not just yet and he most certainly was not interested in their hard-earned gold.

'I seen the likes of you before,' said the other man. 'I'd say you was a preacher. Only preachers wear fancy clothes like that. You ain't no gold-prospector that's for sure.'

'The Reverend Caleb Black,' Caleb introduced himself. 'Bound for Gold Poison City, wherever that is.'

'Another day's ridin',' said the first prospector. 'Maybe it's as well you ain't lookin' for a claim, there ain't none left, leastways none what's worth workin'.'

'I work the gold claims of the Lord,' said Caleb in his most pious voice. 'I mine for the souls of men.'

'Then you got plenty of scope in Gold Poison,' said the man. 'I ain't so sure as you'll be all that welcome though. I reckon there ain't one of 'em what's interested in religion an' I'm darned sure there ain't a single soul up there worth savin'. The devil would stand a better chance than a preacher.'

'If I only make one man see the truth, it will have been a successful foray,' intoned Caleb.

'Gold is the only truth up there,' said the other man. 'Leastways it was, only trouble is it's startin' to run out now, that's why we left.'

'I trust your visit was worthwhile and profitable,' said Caleb. The men bridled slightly which confirmed that they did have gold or money, so Caleb changed the subject. 'I'm curious,' he continued. 'How on earth did it come to have the name Gold Poison City?'

'I guess you could say it was given to it by another preacher,' said the one. 'He turned up just after gold was found an' set about preachin' the evils of money an' greed. He said gold was a poison which burned away at the souls of men, or somethin' like that. Anyway, the name sort of took on an' stuck, so now it's called Gold Poison City.'

'What happened to him?' Caleb asked.

'They strung him up,' replied the other man. 'He offered everybody who gave him their gold everlastin' salvation. He claimed it was a great sacrifice on his part since he would be takin' on the sins of everybody an' would probably be condemned to everlastin' torment himself.'

'You mean he tried to take their gold?'

'That's about it,' said the man with a broad grin. 'It

26

wasn't so much him takin' gold anybody chose to give him, an' believe me there was some who did just that, you could say he got greedy too. They reckoned he was stealin' gold. Don't know for sure if he was or not, but most thought he was so they strung him up. He's buried somewheres up there.'

'Hope you ain't got the same idea,' said the other man. 'Don't know if you know anythin' about minin' towns or not, but there's two things what's guaranteed to get a man strung up. The one is stealin' another man's gold an' the other is claim jumpin'. You can kill a man in a game of cards an' nobody ain't goin' to bother. You can even steal a man's woman, but take a man's gold an' you is sure to die. Your trial takes about five minutes an' it takes another five minutes to string you up.'

'I'll remember that,' said Caleb. 'By the way, I believe two friends of mine headed this way recently. A white man named Billy McGovern and a black man called Leroy Smith. Have you seen them by any chance?'

'Nope,' asserted the one. 'That don't mean nothin' though. There must be a couple of thousand men or more up there. There's all shapes, sizes an' all colours. There's whites, blacks, browns an' yellers. Nobody don't give a damn about the colour of a man's skin, what his religion is, who he is or where he comes from. Anyhow, I doubt if there's one man what uses his real name an' the name Smith . . . why, there must be hundreds of 'em. I'm a Smith myself as far as them up there are concerned. My partner here is a Brown.' Both men laughed.

'Just as I thought,' said Caleb. 'Well, thank you, gentlemen, I'll be on my way. Another day you say?' The men nodded.

Gold Poison proved to be more or less as Caleb had been led to expect. It consisted of a vast expanse of tents and makeshift huts set in a narrow valley. Long before he actually reached the *city* itself, he passed a large number of mine-workings. Some consisted of tunnels dug into the side of the mountain whilst others were simply men digging down into the earth on small plots.

In many cases the plots were very small, perhaps ten or fifteen feet square and the whole site bore a resemblance to many tall, mud-built buildings. This was due to the fact that some of the workings were deeper than others, creating a scene of many towers. It was plain that plot boundaries were rigorously enforced when he heard a man warning his neighbour that he was digging into *his* plot and that he'd kill him if he took so much as another inch. The offender denied this and it seemed that a confrontation was looming. Caleb did not wait to find out what happened.

Those who had chosen to dig into the mountainside had, for the most part, either a tent or shack erected on the site but those with single small plots did not have the room to erect either a tent or a building of any kind. There was water everywhere and rickety-looking sluices criss-crossed the entire valley.

Gold Poison City itself was spreadeagled either side of a now dirty, litter-strewn river and both river and town were more like an open sewer. The stench of human waste was overpowering. There were indeed far more men about than he had seen in a long time.

A solitary, timber-built building attracted his attention and he twisted his way amongst the tents to reach it. There was no sign of anything which might be a road though, everywhere was mud. It seemed that tents were pitched wherever there was enough space, including on the mud.

He tried looking for horses which might belong to the outlaws but, although there were many sorry-looking horses, it was impossible to tell if any of them belonged to the outlaws.

He eventually reached the solitary building and was not at all surprised to discover that it housed a bar, a whorehouse and a mining-supplies store which also sold grocery items, all at vastly inflated prices. There was also a small assay office, seemingly attached as an afterthought, which was also where all claims had to be registered. Opposite this building were a series of larger tents which appeared to be either bars or eating houses. At least that was what the signs proclaimed. It seemed that the eating houses were manned entirely by Chinese.

He entered the wooden building and was immediately accosted by a tired looking woman who offered him a good time for twenty dollars or the equivalent in gold. He politely refused and went up to the crowded bar where he ordered a beer. It cost five dollars a glass and tasted warm and foul. He passed it on to a nearby drunk who did not seem to mind what he drank.

'I know it's a stupid question to ask,' said Caleb to the bartender who turned out to be the owner. 'But I'm looking for two men, one white, one black. They probably rode in a few days ago. They wouldn't look like prospectors.'

'You're right,' grunted the bartender, 'it is a stupid question. Take a look about, what do you see? There's black men, white men an' most other colours. Most ain't real prospectors, they come here hopin' for some easy money but they is always disappointed. There's folk comin' an' goin' all the time so unless a man's ten foot tall, got a hunch back, glass eyes, three legs an' green hair there ain't nobody goin' to look at him twice.'

Caleb did look around but although he knew the faces of the outlaws, there was nobody who looked remotely like them. The only thing of which he was reasonably certain was that they would not turn to prospecting. He was beginning to wonder if he had made one of his rare misjudgements.

'What do most men do who haven't got a claim?' Caleb asked.

'Bum around lookin' for casual work,' replied the bartender. 'Sometimes they get lucky but most times they don't. If your friends ain't got no claim then the most likely place they'll be is in here or one of the other bars or maybe in one of the gamin'-tents. They is best avoided if you got a lick of sense. Run by professional gamblers an' I ain't never seen one of them lose yet. There's a couple of places what provide girls, they could be there.'

'And where do such men find a bed?' Caleb asked.

'Them what can afford it can get a bed in one of the roomin'-houses as they call themselves,' said the bartender. 'All you get for your money is a bed an' a mattress, but no blankets, in a tent along with about thirty others. The price is complete with bedbugs an' lice. Not that bedbugs an' lice seem to bother most folk. Standard charge is five dollars a night. Strange thing is they is almost always full. Strictly cash in advance.'

'It would seem that Gold Poison City is a very expensive place to live,' observed Caleb.

'Supply an' demand,' said the bartender. 'They demand, we supply.'

'And probably far more proftable than grubbing for gold,' said Caleb. 'I don't suppose you provide accommodation?'

'Nope,' replied the bartender, firmly. 'I tried it at first but it was more trouble than it's worth. We're open twenty-four hours a day, seven days a week an' there's always girls available whatever the time of day. The girls charge twenty dollars for fifteen minutes, you go over that, you pay for an extra fifteen minutes.'

'I don't think so,' said Caleb. 'I don't think I fancy any of the so-called rooming-houses either. Thank you for your trouble, I'll see if I can find anywhere outside of town. I don't mind sleeping out in the open.'

'You an' hundreds of others,' observed the bartender.

Caleb left the building and was immediately met by the smell of cooking, which reminded him how hungry he was. He peered into two eating-houses and decided against both but the third was slightly less crowded and the food did smell a little more appetizing. A chalked board outside advertised – in bad English – bare stakes, beef stakes and dere stakes, each costing ten dollars. There was also meat stew, but the type of meat was not specified. That cost eight dollars. It was pure extortion but unless he found his own food, there was little choice but to pay. He decided to risk a 'beef stake'.

The meat proved surprisingly good and well cooked, even if its advanced state of maturity was begining to be obvious. It came with an assortment of vegetables which could have been almost anything but still tasted quite reasonable. Real coffee, he was informed by the little

Chinese man who served him, was five dollars extra. What the man called 'prairie coffee' was only one dollar. Caleb decided to forgo the luxury of either. He had his own supply and would brew some up later. He had tasted 'prairie coffee' a few times before and knew it to be a brew of odd, crushed seeds and leaves and often given added colour by the addition of dyes or even crushed insects.

He led his horse out of Gold Poison and along the river in the opposite direction to that from which he had entered. At first there were the usual blocks of small claims being worked but these soon disappeared when he came to a series of rapids. Everywhere was bare rock and although there were a few hardy types panning the river for gold, most other signs of mining disappeared.

Once past the rapids he soon discovered that he was not alone in trying to find a place to stay for the night. There must have been at least 200 other men, mostly in pairs, along with mules or horses. Some had erected tents but most simply sat out in the open or, if they were lucky, in the lee of rocks.

He climbed a little higher and was most surprised to find an apparently vacant spot almost surrounded by large rocks which gave good shelter. There was also a good expanse of grass for his horse. Clean water was no problem. At that point the river had not become a dumping ground for waste. He soon had a fire going and made himself a welcome coffee.

As he supped at his hot coffee, Caleb considered his next move. Even if the two outlaws were in Gold Poison, the chances of seeing them were remote and the chances of anyone else knowing them even more remote. The odds against anyone recognizing them from his description were also far too long to be of any hope. In any case, he doubted very much if anyone would admit to seeing them. They would not want to become involved. In many other places, a black man and a white man together would have stood out, but here he had seen several such associations, some even with their arms round each other's necks. They might have been drunk but none of them would have been so intimate in other places.

However, despite the seemingly high odds against him, Caleb still had the feeling that his quarry was close by. There was no particular reason, it was simply a gut feeling. He decided to give it at least one more day of searching. If, by the end of that time he had not found them, he would continue towards Morgan City and, if necessary, wait for them there.

About an hour after Caleb had settled down, it started to rain. A man close by told him that it rained most days in the valley. Something to do with the prevailing wind and the high mountain peaks. The man was obviously better educated than most and certainly appeared to know what he was talking about but the technicalities were lost on Caleb.

He donned his waterproof coat and huddled in the lee of the rocks. It appeared that he was in for a wet, uncomfortable night.

THREE

It did not rain all night and according to Caleb's pocket watch, it eventually stopped at two in the morning. He was able to get a few hours' sleep although he discovered that his choice of resting place had turned into a large pool as water cascaded off the surrounding mountain, between the rocks, and he was forced to move a few yards. He decided that he would have to find somewhere else to spend the next night. He now realized just why the plot had not been occupied.

Dawn broke late in the valley simply because the surrounding mountains hid the sun. When it did eventually become light enough really to see what was happening, most of his neighbours were trudging off towards Gold Poison. His educated neighbour had apparently left a lot earlier.

He did manage to locate enough dry wood to make a fire and brew himself another coffee. He was in no great hurry, he would wait a little longer to make certain that everyone was up and about.

He had just thrown the dregs of his coffee on to the fire when he suddenly became aware that he was being watched. Without raising his head to make it obvious that he knew, he simply raised his eyes slightly. What he saw made him instinctively drop his hand to his side close to one of his two guns.

There was no doubt about it, Billy McGovern and Leroy Smith, also with guns in hand, were no more than five yards away and staring straight at him.

'Well now,' drawled Smith. 'Seems to me we met somewheres else before. You followin' us, Preacher Man?'

'I beg your pardon?' queried Caleb, aware that any attempt to draw his gun would result in his instant death. 'I don't think we've ever met.' He quite deliberately pretended not to know who they were. 'The Reverend Caleb Black,' he continued, introducing himself. 'And you are?'

'Don't matter none who we are, Reveren',' said Smith. 'Sure, we met before an' not that long ago either. Back in Burney it was, in the saloon. We saw you yesterday comin' out of one of them eatin'-houses.'

'Burney, in the saloon?' queried Caleb. He suddenly smiled and nodded. 'Ah, yes, I remember now. There were more of you then, though, at least I seem to recall there were at least six of you.' He was also quite deliberately vague about the exact number and once again he smiled and nodded. 'There was a certain amount of excitement, but I don't think you were around at the time. Apparently somebody tried to rob the bank.'

'Did they now?' said McGovern. 'Did you happen to see who?'

'No, I did not,' said Caleb. 'I might be a minister but I have no particular liking for the law. Being a stranger in the town I thought they might think I was somehow involved but I convinced the sheriff that I was simply passing through. I left almost immediately after the attempted robbery. I do believe the robbers were killed though, but I didn't hang about to make sure.' He nodded at their guns. 'Please, gentlemen, put those weapons away. Guns make me nervous.'

He had pulled his long coat over his two guns in the hope that they would not see them. It seemed that they had not. They both smiled and slid their guns into their holsters.

'And what brings you into this god-forsaken hole, Reveren'?' asked Smith. 'Nobody in his right mind would come here.'

'Precisely that,' said Caleb. 'A god-forsaken hole if ever I saw one. I am a preacher and a minister. What better place to save a few souls? Whether or not I am in my right mind is, I suppose, open to question. The same thing could be said of you. Actually, I had never heard of the place. I just happened to see a sign on the road to Morgan City. With such a strange name I couldn't resist coming to see what sort of place Gold Poison City was.'

They both laughed. 'Now there's a coincidence, same here,' said McGovern. 'So now we all know what kind of place it is an' I reckon we all think we've wasted our time. I ain't never been to a gold town before, never been interested an' I ain't so sure I ever want to see one again. Seems to me a man needs to find a hell of a lot of gold to even be able to afford to live out here. You know what they charge for a small glass of beer – an' foul stuff it is as well?'

'Five dollars,' said Caleb. 'I agree, it was just about

the worst beer I've ever tasted. Heaven only knows what they charge for whiskey or gin. Not that I ever drink either, but it certainly couldn't taste worse than the beer.'

'Everythin's the same price,' said Smith. 'Five dollars a shot for whiskey, rum an' gin. Only one what tastes like the genuine thing is the rum an' I reckon that's watered down. The whiskey is raw enough to take the back off your throat. Where you headed for now, Reveren'? On to Morgan City?'

'Being a complete stranger to this part of the world, I'm not sure,' said Caleb. 'It would seem that this Morgan City is the only place of any size. It most certainly cannot be any worse than this place.'

'What about savin' a few sinners here?' said McGovern with a wry laugh. 'I reckon they all need it. You could set up a business savin' souls for ten dollars a time.'

'Apparently there was another minister who had that idea,' said Caleb. 'I believe his body is buried close by. No, having seen the place I will willingly concede this place as a defeat for Christianity and a victory for the devil. The odds are too powerful, something like two or three thousand to one against me, I would guess. I like a challenge but not this much of a challenge.'

'OK, Reveren',' said Smith. 'Just thought we'd check you out. We get kind of nervous when we see folk what seem to be followin' us. Maybe we'll see you in Morgan City sometime.'

'Quite possibly,' said Caleb.

He was going to suggest that they ride to Morgan City together but decided that he did not want to appear too friendly or arouse any suspicion. However, he now knew where they were going. He would follow and bide his time.

One thing was quite certain. Gold Poison was most certainly not a place to attempt to arrest anyone or to chance any heroics. It was quite possible the entire population would be on the side of McGovern and Smith. That apart, there was nowhere for him to take the outlaws should he arrest them. He had been wondering just how many other wanted outlaws were hiding there. He had no doubts that there were quite a few. However, having set his sights on McGovern and Smith, he was not interested in anyone else.

Caleb packed up his few belongings and wandered back to the town. He now intended leaving that morning but decided that he had better find out which was the shortest way to Morgan City.

The aroma from the eating-house he had dined at before told him that it would be as well if he ate before he left. There was no knowing where or when he would find his next meal. The choice was exactly the same as it had been the previous evening so once again he opted for 'beef stake'. Having eaten, he went into the wooden building and the bar.

Once again he was approached by a haggard-looking woman and once again he refused. The man who owned the place was apparently still in bed but the bartender on duty assured him that the only way to Morgan City was to follow a well-worn trail over the mountain. That road, he was assured, was the way supplies were brought in. The trail started almost immediately behind the wooden building.

He was outside and about to leave when sudden panic seemed to grip the entire population. The cry went up that 'Warlock' was heading for town. Men were running in all directions obviously intent on hiding themselves. The bartender appeared at Caleb's side. He seemed very worried.

' "Warlock"?' asked Caleb. 'Who in God's name is "Warlock" and why is everybody so scared?'

'US Marshal Sam Warlock,' said the bartender, obviously very concerned. 'If he's true to form, he's got at least ten deputies with him. Believe me, mister, it don't pay to be around when Warlock's payin' one of his visits. The Devil, that's what they call him an' devil he is too. Comes here about once every two months lookin' for wanted men an' outlaws. Mostly we hear he's on the way, which gives us time to hide somewheres, but sometimes he just suddenly arrives. This is one of them times, he's taken everybody by surprise. He was here only two weeks ago so folk weren't expectin' him so soon.' He looked up and down the valley and licked his lips.

'It ain't no good anybody thinkin' they can run,' he continued. 'Warlock always sends at least two deputies to either end of the valley before he comes into town. That way anybody what does try to run ends up either bein' arrested or killed. Usually they gets killed an' it don't matter to Warlock if they is wanted men or not. He says that only a guilty man needs to run an' he's probably right. In fact they do say he prefers dead men, they cause less trouble.'

'Then I suggest that you make yourself scarce,' said Caleb, looking hard at the man. 'You obviously have no desire to meet him.'

'No, sir,' agreed the bartender. 'There's only fifty dollars out on me, but that don't matter to Warlock. He'd take a man if there was only fifty cents out on him. I'll say this for him, he's good, very good. He's got a memory what can place a man even if there ain't no picture of him. It's almost as if he can smell the price on a man's head.'

Caleb had never heard of Marshal Sam Warlock, but he was very plainly well known to the residents of Gold Poison City and already most were making themselves scarce, even those whom Caleb was certain did not have a price on their heads. It seemed that even the innocent were scared of Sam Warlock.

Caleb immediately thought of McGovern and Smith. If Warlock was only half as good as the bartender claimed, the chances were that he would somehow find the two outlaws. He knew that flyers were in circulation describing the men. If that happened, Caleb knew that he could say farewell to any hope of collecting the reward money. Although it went against the grain, Caleb realized that the only chance he had of collecting was to help the pair avoid the clutches of the marshal and collect on them at a later date. He tethered his horse outside the building, removed his rifle and started to search for the two outlaws.

Another shout went up that two men had been shot trying to escape along the southern route out of the valley and Caleb had the sinking feeling that they might be McGovern and Smith. However, he still continued his search. It appeared that even all work on claims had ceased, such was the effect of the presence of Marshal Sam Warlock and his deputies.

Caleb eventually returned to the bar and then found himself at the rear of the building where, much to his relief, he saw the two outlaws. They were doing their best to hide amongst piles of rubbish.

At the side of the building, Caleb had seen several wooden crates and he had noticed that at least one of them was empty and that the lid to it was close by. An idea quickly formed in his mind. He looked carefully around and waited for a moment while a deputy passed by searching various tents.

'Over here!' he called. 'If you want to avoid the marshal, just do as I say. It's obvious from the way you're acting that you don't want him to see you. I don't know why that should be so, but I'm no lover of the law either so I don't really care. I think I can save you.'

'An' why the hell should you do that, Preacher Man?' demanded Smith. 'Why should you care what happens to us?'

'I don't,' said Caleb. 'OK, if you don't want my help, I'll leave you to Warlock. Do you know him?'

'I know him,' said McGovern. 'He knows me too. OK, we admit it, we got prices on our heads. We're willin' to listen.'

'Then follow me,' ordered Caleb.

Going ahead to make certain that there were no more deputies around, he led them to the side of the building and the wooden crates. He ordered them to climb inside an empty crate. It was cramped but, faced with no other option, they obeyed. Caleb then replaced the damaged lid and draped a canvas sheet over end. He was taking care to make it appear to anyone walking by the crate that, although plainly open, it was otherwise undisturbed, hence the the canvas sheet over one end. Once he was satisfied, Caleb leant against the crate and waited.

He did not have to wait too long before three men, each dressed in long, heavy, waterproof coats and carrying rifles, appeared. They stared hard at Caleb as if not quite believing their eyes. Perhaps wondering why he had not fled along with everyone else. One of them nodded to the other two, who raised their guns at Caleb and then he moved forward and faced Caleb squarely.

'You look like a preacher,' he snarled. 'I reckon even if you didn't know before, by now you probably know who I am. US Marshal Sam Warlock. They do tell me a warlock is some kind of devil man an' believe me, I can be just that an' more when I've a mind to be. Who the hell are you?'

'The Reverend Caleb Black,' said Caleb. He deliberately stood up and started to walk away from the box. He felt that he had done enough to divert attention away from the crate. 'I was about to leave this hell-hole when you arrived. I was told it would be most unwise to be seen attempting to leave whilst you are around. I hear that two men did attempt to escape and that they are now dead. Were they outlaws? My horse is at the front, I hope you don't mind if I do leave now.'

Warlock appeared rather surprised, obviously unused to anyone addressing him in such a way. Caleb continued to lead them well away from the crate The sound of shooting could be heard and Warlock smiled. Caleb assumed that other men had tried to escape.

'Caleb Black!' Warlock suddenly said. 'Yeah, I thought I'd heard the name somewhere before. You've got yourself a reputation already. You ain't no preacher, you're a bounty hunter. I hate all bounty hunters whether they're white or black, you're all scum. I heard about you when I ran into the circuit judge on my way here. Seems you just collected a couple of thousand dollars on some outlaws who tried to rob the bank in Burney. That's nice money.'

'The same,' admitted Caleb. 'However, I can assure you that I *am* also an ordained minister. I have proof of my claim should you wish to see it and I confess to also being a bounty hunter. The reason is really very simple. It's just that I find saving a man's soul who happens to have a price on his head far more satisfying and certainly far more profitable than simply praying for their souls.'

'It's questionable if any outlaws got any souls or not, but you're probably right,' said Warlock. 'I still hate bounty hunters, even if they are preachers. It's the likes of you who take food from the mouths of me an' my deputies. I don't work like other marshals, I get paid by results an' believe me, I always get results.'

'A state sponsored bounty hunter,' observed Caleb. 'Yes, I have met other marshals like you before.'

'There's not many of us,' said Warlock, somewhat proudly. 'I suppose you could call me a bounty hunter, but I have the advantage of being a US marshal. That means I can do things bounty hunters like you can't. I've got the backin' of the law. Now I'm thinkin' that you and me are after the same men. We both know that the two main men in that bank robbery didn't get caught. Leroy Smith an' Billy McGovern. Seein' you up here in Gold Poison makes me think that you're

43

followin' them. Maybe you even know where they are. I'm sure I don't need to tell you, Preacher Man, but if'n I was you I wouldn't tell any of my deputies how much money you've got. They just might mistake you for an outlaw.'

'And you wouldn't do a damned thing about it,' said Caleb. 'Don't you go mistaking me for an outlaw either, I have eyes up my ass.' He pulled aside the front of his coat to reveal both his guns. 'I can use them both equally well,' he continued by way of a warning.

'Now I done seen everythin',' grinned Warlock. 'A two-gun-totin' preacher man. I might be a mean bastard but I don't go murderin' men for their money. You'll just have to hope that you get to McGovern an' Smith before I do if you want that reward.'

'I admit that I did come up here hoping to find them,' said Caleb, 'but it would seem that I was wrong. In the short time I have been here I have seen many men who probably do have prices on their heads. They are probably all small time, maybe a couple of hundred apiece at the most, but those two were certainly not amongst them. Had they been I can assure you I would have spirited them away long before you arrived.'

'Most of 'em ain't worth even that much,' said Warlock. 'Still, even fifty dollars is better'n nothin'.'

By that time other deputies were arriving pushing sorry-looking, mud-covered men in front of them. Four bodies were also carried in. The captives were herded into a small paddock and two deputies put on guard. This continued for the next hour and Caleb stayed around to see just how many would eventually be arrested.

In all there were twenty-three apparent outlaws. Caleb was most surprised to see the educated man who knew all about the weather amongst them. He was not surprised to see the bartender.

When it seemed that they had rounded up all likely outlaws, Warlock barked an order at his deputies who immediately pushed and prodded their captives into the bar. Warlock took a bag off his horse and followed them into the bar. In the absence of instructions to the contrary, a curious Caleb also followed.

The captives were forced to line up and Warlock grinned evilly at them as he slammed the bag on to a table. He nodded at Caleb as if enjoying having an audience and opened the bag. He took out a sheaf of papers and once again grinned evilly at the men lined up before him. The educated man and the bartender were on the end of the line.

'Those two I have seen before,' Caleb said casually to Warlock. 'That one . . .' he nodded at the bartender, 'has a price of fifty dollars on him. That other one . . .' he nodded at the educated man, 'I am rather surprised at. Are you certain he's an outlaw?'

Warlock grunted, walked up to the educated man and stared hard at him. He then returned to his sheaf of wanted posters and thumbed through them. He suddenly gave a satisfied grunt.

'Outlaw?' he said to Caleb. 'Well now, that depends on what you mean by *outlaw*. Unless I'm very much mistaken you're Jonathan Broadbent,' he said to the man. 'Don't try to deny it, I ain't never wrong.' He turned to Caleb. 'He's not an outlaw in the sense that he makes his livin' murderin' an' robbin'. He murdered his wife an' her sister back in Phoenix. Been on the run for a year now. His wife's family put up the money for his capture, dead or alive. Didn't expect to find him here though, it's way off his territory. That's what I like about this job, the unexpected, like meetin' you. Yes, sir, Mr Broadbent is worth a thousand dollars to me.' He once again walked along the line of glowering men, stopping occasionally to say something to one of them. He eventually walked back to Caleb.

'He certainly looks like Broadbent,' said Caleb, examining the poster. 'Are you Jonathan Broadbent?' he said to the man.

'There does not seem to be a lot of point in denying it,' agreed the man. 'I didn't realize my details would reach this far. Yes, sir, I am he.'

For the next hour, Caleb watched fascinated as Sam Warlock carefully examined his posters and the men lined up and questioned them. In most cases he hardly needed the posters and the men admitted their identities. In a few cases the men insisted that they were not outlaws, that their names were either Smith, Brown, Green or Jones and that it was a case of mistaken identity. Out of the twenty-three, which included the four dead men, fourteen proved to have rewards out on them. Two of the dead men did not appear to be outlaws, but that fact certainly did not appear to bother Sam Warlock.

Eventually and seemingly satisfied, Warlock told those he could not prove to be outlaws that they could go. At the same time he warned them that he was very good at remembering faces and that if they did have something to hide, they would be better off leaving his territory. He did not specify the boundaries of 'his' territory.

The twelve men detained, along with the bodies of the two outlaws, were herded outside and into one of the so-called rooming-houses. The owner of the business protested loudly, demanding payment for the beds occupied and even those left empty by deserting customers. Sam Warlock answered the man by ramming his long barrelled Colt up the man's nose. There was no need for the marshal to say anything. The man simply fled.

Seemingly from nowhere, three of the deputies produced leg-irons which were clamped to each man's ankles, each being joined by a short chain which allowed the captives to shuffle along. Then, all the men had their hands tied to the wooden bed-frames and four deputies were posted at each corner of the tent. Sam Warlock obviously did not take any chances.

The other deputies, after being given a guard roster, were told the time was their own and they immediately celebrated by charging into the bar, helping themselves to drink and grabbing the few luckless women who had remained. It was very noticeable that the owner of the bar did not protest. For the remainder of the night they either stood guard, took turns with the women or became much the worse for drink.

'Not a bad day's work,' Warlock said almost gleefully to Caleb some time later. 'Broadbent alone is worth a thousand dollars and all in all this little lot is worth about three thousand dollars.'

'If there's ten of you, that's only three hundred apiece,' observed Caleb. 'I suppose that's not too bad, but it'd be better if it was all yours.'

'That's not how things work,' said Warlock. 'I take the highest reward for myself, then the rest is divided between us all, me included. Most don't like the arrangement but that's their tough luck. They're all worse scum than the men we catch, but they ain't got no prices on their heads, leastways not that I knows to. They work for me under those terms or they don't work at all. I reckon they probably earn about two hundred dollars a month most months, which is one hell of a lot easier an' more'n they could earn diggin' dirt for gold or chasin' cows. It's been a good month so far, they've earned almost four hundred.'

'So you take the one thousand out on Broadbent plus a share in the others,' said Caleb. 'That makes more sense.'

'Sure does,' agreed Warlock. 'I reckon that another twelve months will see me rich enough to retire. None of this lot will ever be able to retire. All they're interested in is drink, gamblin' an' women. But then I suppose that's obvious. I wouldn't trust any one of 'em not to kill me if he thought I had money on me. That's why I told you not to let it be known how much money you have. They're all heathens so killin' a preacher won't mean nothin'. I make it a point never to carry more'n about ten dollars on me. I take this lot back to Rockwood, collect my money an' pay it straight into a bank.'

'Rockwood?' queried Caleb.

'State penitentiary, about thirty miles south-west of Morgan City,' explained Warlock. 'That's my base, not that I'm there very often. OK, Mr Preacher Man, you're free to go whenever you want. Don't bank on gettin' that bounty off McGovern an' Smith though.'

'I won't,' assured Caleb. 'Bank on it, I mean.'

'Good,' said Warlock. 'There's one thing you ought to know about bounty huntin' in my territory. I don't allow it. Nobody but me gets the reward due off any outlaw. No exceptions, not even bounty huntin' preachers. Do I make myself clear?' He did not give Caleb the opportunity to reply as he strode off.

FOUR

Caleb did not have any time to check on the two men in the crate because there were too many prying eyes. When he finally left the bar and was satisfied that there were no deputies around, he went round the side of the building but it was obvious that the crate was now empty. The lid was on the ground along with the canvas sheet. He was not really surprised and he was quite certain that by that time they were heading away from Gold Poison City as fast as they possibly could. He could only hope that they were heading for Morgan City.

He decided to delay his own departure until the following morning. There were only about two hours of daylight remaining and he certainly did not like the idea of attempting the road through the forest and over the mountain in the dark. Neither the darkness nor the mountains bothered Caleb, but during his short stay in Gold Poison he had heard tales of numerous bears in the forest. In truth, Caleb had something of a morbid fear of bears. He could not explain this fear so he avoided bear country wherever possible. Despite their start, he felt reasonably sure that he would have little difficulty in locating the two outlaws again.

Finding somewhere to sleep that night proved far easier than it had the previous night and thankfully it did not rain during the night. He was awake at the first sign of the breaking dawn.

He thought about having something to eat before he left, but soon discovered that all the eating-houses were closed. He was not really surprised since the deputies had taken full advantage of their largely assumed authority during the previous night and refused to pay for food. The owners of the eating-houses probably thought it would be wiser to wait until the marshal and his deputies had departed before reopening.

He went to find Marshal Sam Warlock and was very surprised that there was no sign of him, any of the deputies or their prisoners. He was told by the disgruntled owner of the bar that they had departed just before dawn, most of them having spent the entire night drinking his stock of liquor and with his girls, again, services for which they did not pay. Caleb checked that the trail leading up the mountain from behind the bar *was* the road to Morgan City and he too left Gold Poison City, vowing never to return.

There appeared to be two tracks up the mountain. The one went more or less straight up and was very steep and muddy. The second seemed to take a more meandering, zig zag route and was plainly the easiest and most well-used. It was this route which Caleb opted to take.

There were one or two others also leaving Gold Poison but they did not look like prospectors and few carried the tools associated with prospecting. They gave the impression of being more like disillusioned chancers. Most were walking. Horses and even mules were plainly too expensive for them and the few who had arrived with such animals had probably sold them or lost them in card-games.

Caleb was almost at the top of the road when he came across Marshal Sam Warlock and his bedraggled, sorry-looking entourage. Jonathan Broadbent gave him a weak, sad smile and the bartender with fifty dollars his head stared at him glumly. Caleb felt quite sorry for the two of them. The prisoners were now shackled together in pairs, one set of leg-irons joining two men. The bodies of the two dead outlaws were across a mule.

'Are you walking them all the way back to Rockwood?' Caleb asked as he drew alongside the marshal. 'That must be one hell of a long walk.'

'Nope,' said Warlock. 'There's a railroad down the other side. We walk as far as that. I've got a train waitin' to take me direct to Rockwood.'

'That sounds like a good idea,' said Caleb. 'Does the train go through Morgan City?'

'Not this one,' said Warlock. 'Morgan City train is in two days. Nearest this one goes is to Taylor's Junction, about thirty miles from Morgan City.'

'And how far is it from here to Morgan City?'

'Maybe sixty miles,' said the marshal. 'Anyhow, this one ain't a regular passenger train. It's for my own private use. There's a wagon for our horses, one for the prisoners, one for my deputies an' a carriage for me. I like to travel in comfort and alone. You can follow McGovern an' Smith for all the good it'll do you. They can't be too far ahead. Maybe you'll catch 'em before I do but it won't do you no good. Just remember what I said.'

'I don't see why,' said Caleb. 'I never saw them in Gold Poison.'

'You didn't?' said the marshal, giving Caleb a knowing smile. 'Oh, they was there all right. Believe me, I knows they was there.'

Caleb could not help but return the knowing smile and decided it was probably better not to try and convince the marshal otherwise or to travel with him or to argue about the bounty. He gave him a brief nod and spurred on his horse.

On the way down, Caleb passed more people leaving Gold Poison, again many of them on foot but a few others with loaded mules. The ones with mules looked like prospectors, which was probably why they still had their mules. He tried asking some of them if they had seen McGovern and Smith but the only response from most of them was a sour glower.

When he eventually reached flat ground, he came across the marshal's train in a siding at what appeared to be a small railroad station. There was no obvious reason for the station but Caleb did not believe that it was to service Gold Poison. There was a large pile of logs and a water tower which indicated it was nothing more than a refuelling stop.

The engine was in the process of building up steam but the engineer proved a little more co-operative than the other men drifting away from Gold Poison. He confirmed that two men matching Caleb's description had passed by. It had been close to midnight the previous night and had therefore been dark, but there was no mistaking that one was a white man and the other a black man. Apparently the engineer hardly ever took to his bed before midnight. He also confirmed that they had taken the road to Morgan City.

At first the road followed a series of thickly wooded, steep, narrow valleys and small rivers but by mid-afternoon it opened up on to flatter, more rolling countryside. During that time Caleb had been on the look-out for signs that his quarry had stopped, but there was nothing obvious. In any case, it would have been a simple matter for them to ride off the main trail and become invisible. It was quite possible that he might have passed them and not known it. All he could do was to continue towards Morgan City and hope to find them there.

He tried to recall the maps he had seen in Burney and it seemed to him that there was nowhere else anyone could go. To the north, he recalled, it led up into the mountains, to the south into cattle-ranching country and to the west, eventually into desert. At least he seemed to remember something about a desert. However, he knew that his memory on such matters was far from perfect. He had most certainly missed the fact that Rockwood even existed and was not that far from Morgan City.

Later that afternoon he managed to shoot a small deer and just before dusk made camp alongside a large, clear pool set amongst some rocks. There he also found signs that he was not the first to camp alongside the pool. There were the remains of many fires, most obviously quite old, but one plainly very recent. He could only guess as to whether or not McGovern and Smith had stayed there. It proved to be a surprisingly cold night and Caleb was forced to keep the fire going all through the night.

It was approaching midday when Caleb saw a thin column of smoke rising above some trees about 200 yards off the road. Out of little more than idle curiosity, he decided to investigate.

He pulled up amongst a group of trees from where he looked down on two men in the apparent process of searching a body. There was no doubt that the two men were McGovern and Smith. The body on the ground looked very much like a prospector. A fire was still burning close to the body.

Caleb slowly moved forward and was surprised at just how close to the men he was able to get. He seriously considered taking out the two outlaws there and then. Killing both of them would have been a fairly simple matter. However, he wanted them alive and decided that it would have been too risky and too much of a problem to take them alive at that moment. He would bide his time. When they did see him they immediately grabbed their guns but when they realized who he was, they relaxed but it was noticeable that they did not put their guns away.

'Well now, if it ain't the preacher man,' drawled Smith. 'I guess we owe you. Good idea of yours hidin' in that crate. Sorry we didn't hang about but it didn't seem such a good idea.'

'At least it fooled Warlock,' said Caleb. 'What happened here? It looks like you just murdered a prospector.'

'Maybe that's what it looks like,' said McGovern. 'We never laid a hand on him though. See for yourself. We saw him, he saw us an' then he suddenly just collapsed. He's dead, dropped dead, just like that. First time I ever seen a man just drop dead for no reason. I've seen men die when they've been shot, but never just 'cos he died for no reason.'

Caleb dismounted and examined the body. The age of the man was, as with most elderly, bearded prospectors, difficult to ascertain. He could have been any age between fifty and eighty. There were certainly no marks or signs of any violence and he was forced to concede that the man had apparently died of natural causes.

'Probably a heart attack,' he said. 'I've seen it before. So why are you searching his body?'

'Well, we figured it this way,' said Smith. 'He looks like a prospector an' the chances are that prospectors have gold. Since he ain't got no use for it no longer, I figured we'd put it to good use.'

'And did you find any?' asked Caleb.

'Just this,' said Smith, holding up a small leather pouch. 'Sure don't seem that much to me, not much more'n a few nuggets an' a bit of dust.' He threw the pouch to Caleb who emptied it into his hand and studied it.

'I'm no expert on the price of gold,' said Caleb, 'but I'd say there was not much more than twenty or thirty dollars' worth, maybe fifty dollars at most. Not much to show for all that digging.' He put the gold back in the pouch and tossed it back to Smith. 'Is there anything on him to say who he was?'

'There's an old letter,' said McGovern. 'Don't mean much to either of us though. Leroy can't read at all an' I can't read good enough to work out what it says. Anyhow, it's in proper handwritin' an' I can only read things in big letters.' He handed the letter to Caleb.

'You read it, I reckon you is an educated man. You've sure had more book-learnin' than either of us. Anyhow, you're just the man he needs right now. You're a preacher an' preachers is somebody to give him a decent, proper burial.'

Caleb read the letter and said that the man's name was apparently Jed and that the letter was from the man's wife whose name was Elizabeth. There was an address in one of the Eastern states.

'I think she ought to have what little gold there is,' he said. 'I'll take him on to Morgan City and sort things out.'

'An' keep the gold for yourself,' sneered Smith. 'No, sir, Mr Preacher Man. It might not be much but we'll keep it.'

'You don't trust me?' observed Caleb.

Billy McGovern laughed. 'No, sir, we don't trust you. OK, so you put Warlock off findin' us an' we is more'n grateful for that, but I for one just don't understand why you did it. We ain't nothin' to you, we never saw you before Burney an' you never saw us. I'd say you couldn't give a damn what happens to us. I knows we sure as hell couldn't care less what happens to you. We're outlaws an' you know it. I might not be too bright when it comes to book-learnin' but I been around long enough to know when somebody's got other motives. I reckon you knew it was us what planned that bank robbery back in Burney an' that it wasn't just chance what took you to Gold Poison. I think you was lookin' for us.'

'And why should I do that?' asked Caleb.

'Darned if I know,' said McGovern. 'But there's

somethin' about you what just don't sit right with me. A real preacher man you might be but I don't think you helped us simply because you wanted to save our souls an' I sure as hell don't believe it's because you don't like the law.'

'He's right,' said Smith. 'We've had plenty of time to talk an' it was mostly about you. We can't either of us figure out just what you want from us an' frankly we don't care. You do what you like with this body, we is goin' on to Morgan City an' we is goin' alone. Thanks for what you've done for us, but I don't feel comfortable with you about. Do I make myself clear, *Reveren'*?'

'Perfectly,' said Caleb, with a broad grin. 'Just one thing. I talked to Marshal Warlock before I left Gold Poison and somehow he seems to know that you were both in there. He also told me there's a large reward out on you both and that he intends to collect. I think he means it. He's taking those prisoners back to a place called Rockwood—'

'I know it,' interrupted McGovern. 'I ought to, I did three years in prison there. That's where I got to know Warlock.'

'Then I would have thought that Morgan City was not a place for you to go,' said Caleb. 'He will probably search for you there and he does appear to be a very thorough and determined man.'

'We'll chance it,' said McGovern. 'Morgan City is a big place an' a man can get himself lost easy enough if'n he's got a mind to. 'Sides, I got me some unfinished business there.'

'Unfinished business,' said Caleb. 'Now that sounds to me that you intend to kill somebody. That's what "unfinished business" usually means.'

'Think what you've a mind to, Preacher Man,' snapped McGovern. 'We is grateful to you for what you've done, but don't try pushin' your luck.'

The fact that both men had taken a slightly tighter grip on their guns persuaded Caleb not to push his luck. Apart from the rifle in his saddle holster, about which neither man had made any comment, his two Colt pistols were deliberately well hidden under his long coat. It would have been impossible for him to draw either gun before they shot him. If nothing else, the Reverend Caleb Black did not take unnecessary chances, especially when his own life was at stake.

Both men laughed, mounted their horses and did not give Caleb any opportunity to use his two guns. Their mistrust appeared to extend to making certain that he was well covered by their guns. They laughed again and rode off.

Caleb watched them disappear before turning his attention to the dead man. Once again he carefully examined the body and again could find no obvious cause of death.

As his first examination had shown, the exact age of the man was impossible to determine and the best Caleb could come up with was his first estimate of somewhere between fifty years of age and eighty years of age. He also discovered another letter which once again proved to have been written by the man's wife, this time urging him to go back home.

The one thing which did surprise Caleb was the lack of gold or even money on the body. The man certainly appeared to have all the right equipment for prospecting and, even allowing for the vastly inflated prices of goods in Gold Poison, he would have expected rather more in the way of gold or even cash. He even felt the body for a money-belt, but there was nothing.

Had it been much further to Morgan City, Caleb would probably have buried the body there, but he decided to take the man and report the death to the proper authorities. They might also get a doctor to confirm cause of death.

The man's mule was close by and Caleb checked all the man's belongings just in case the gold was hidden, but it seemed there was no gold. Caleb was still rather puzzled. He did not believe that McGovern and Smith had discovered it, neither man was bright enough to be able to conceal the fact had they done so. After checking all through the man's belongings, Caleb was about to throw the body across the saddle of the mule when he decided to check underneath the saddle.

Removing the heavy, old saddle revealed nothing. and he was about to replace it when he noticed that some stitching on the underside of the saddle was broken. He gently picked at the remaining stitching and soon discovered several, quite large, leather pouches. He opened one and found gold-dust. He guessed at perhaps nine or ten ounces.

He opened up the stitching even more and in total discovered ten pouches, each appearing to contain nine or possibly ten ounces of gold-dust. Hidden deep inside the horn of the saddle he also found a pouch which held a number of gold nuggets, although it was not as heavy as the other pouches.

'Now that's more like it,' he said to himself. 'It would

appear that Jed was quite a wealthy man after all. There might be a hundred or more ounces of gold here. That's more gold than I've ever seen in my life.' He fingered the pouch containing the gold nuggets and smiled to himself. 'All this gold and nobody knows about it,' he mused. 'The devil has some very tempting ways.'

After thoroughly searching the saddle he placed all the pouches in his own saddlebags, loaded Jed's body on to the mule, kicked dirt over the fire and went on his way.

Caleb arrived in Morgan City just as the sun was setting. He was surprised that few people gave him or his cargo a second glance, despite its plainly being a body. It was almost as if such sights were commonplace.

He quickly found the sheriff's office where a bored-looking deputy listened to what he had to say and then made it quite plain that he was not at all interested in the body or who he was. All the more so when it was established that the man had apparently died of natural causes.

'You need a lawyer,' muttered the deputy. 'If there is gold an' you know who he is an' where he comes from, that makes it a civil matter. Civil matters ain't no concern of the likes of me or the sheriff. We've got our hands full enforcin' the peace here in Morgan City.'

'OK,' conceded Caleb. 'Point me in the direction of a lawyer. In the meantime what do I do with the body? I can't carry it around all night.'

'There's plenty of lawyers about,' replied the deputy. 'There's two right across the street. Leastways there would be if their offices were open. Lawyers got it easy, they only work from eight in the mornin' 'til six at night an' don't work Saturdays an' Sundays at all. Today's only Thursday though. They'll be open first thing in the mornin'. As for the body, I guess you're right about takin' it round all night. Not that anybody would bother if you did. Best thing you can do is take it to one of the undertakers.'

'And where might I find an undertaker?' asked Caleb. 'Don't tell me they only work from eight in the morning as well.'

'Nope,' said the deputy with a slight grin, 'I guess since folk don't die only between eight an' six they have to be on hand any time of day or night. Nearest one is down the next street. Saul Bannon is the name. If he can't help, he'll know somebody as can.'

Caleb took the body to Saul Bannon whose first concern was exactly who was responsible for the costs involved. When Caleb produced a twenty-dollar note and asked if that would cover any costs, including burial, Saul Bannon readily agreed and snatched the money from Caleb's grasp, as if fearing that he might change his mind.

The body was taken into a back room and placed in a rough coffin. Caleb was assured that it would be quite safe. Caleb was forced to smile to himself. He hardly expected Jed to walk away in the middle of the night or anyone to break in and steal the body.

Having got rid of the body, Caleb found a livery-stable where he bedded down his horse and agreed a price for the sale of Jed's mule. He carefully removed the gold from his saddlebags, not prepared to take the

62

risk of having it stolen, and spread the pouches amongst various pockets. He then found himself a fairly respectable-looking hotel nearby.

Not wanting to walk about town carrying his rifle, he hid it under the mattress, although he realized that that would be one of the first places an intruder would look, but he had no reason to think that anyone would search his room.

He then decided that he was hungry and since the hotel did not provide meals, he set out to find himself some decent food at one of two places recommended by the hotel-owner and take a look around town in the hope of establishing the whereabouts of Billy McGovern and Leroy Smith. However, he quickly discovered that Morgan City was just coming to life and that what appeared to be the very dregs of humanity were slowly emerging from the surrounding woodwork.

He found what seemed to be a good eating-house, apparently owned and run by a Chinese family. The food was good and not too expensive. A short time later he found himself in what was obviously the centre of the city and which appeared to comprise three main streets running east to west and five other streets running north to south. There were also numerous alleyways down which there seemed to be a steady stream of business of one kind or another.

He calculated that there must have been well over 3,000 people, mostly men, apparently intent on drinking as much as possible, losing as much money as they could in the numerous gaming-saloons and testing out all the whores available in almost every establishment. He realized that his chances of locating McGovern and

Smith were remote, but he persisted.

Morgan City appeared most unlike any other Western town he had encountered. It seemed to be centred on gambling and women. Here it seemed that nobody took any notice of the colour of a man's skin, the only common point of interest was the colour of a man's money. In almost every other town or city he had been in, there had been a definite bias against black men and Indians and of the two the Indian was generally the most despised. It was true that so far he had not seen anyone who was obviously Indian, but he had the feeling that it would not have mattered had there been any providing they could pay their way.

It was also one of the very few occasions when nobody appeared the slightest bit interested or surprised to see a black minister. In fact it was questionable if anyone actually realized he *was* a preacher. A church seemed to be the one building which had no place in Morgan City. He certainly did not see one but he assumed that there were probably a few further out of town in the residential parts. Indeed, God seemed to have no presence at all in the centre of Morgan City. The only god appeared to be money.

On at least three occasions he thought he had located the two outlaws, but on each occasion it proved otherwise. He also started to lose count of the number of deputy sheriffs and eventually worked out that there must be at least six, allowing for the fact that he saw the same one several times, possibly more.

Whether or not it was the presence of the deputies he was unable to work out, but there were surprisingly few fights and those he did see were soon over and done with after a couple of blows.

As well as constantly being harassed by whores on almost every corner, Caleb soon discovered that the alleyways were a source of what were, in his eyes, less natural attractions. A few men touted for customers to witness live sex shows, sex shows involving various animals and, much to his disgust and even more so than the shows with animals, he was offered sex with young girls and young boys, some as young as six or seven years old. He realized that such things did happen, but he had never seen it offered so blatantly. Even worse was the fact that authority apparently did nothing to stop it.

He did question one of the deputies about this more sordid aspect of life in Morgan City, but was met with a resigned shrug and told that in most cases the children involved were Indian. This fact alone seemed to make it acceptable.

Eventually Caleb gave up, there were far too many distractions to searching for the two outlaws and he returned to his hotel. Thankfully it was situated some distance from the main activity of the town and was relatively quiet. He would resume his search the next day when there would be fewer people about and fewer distractions.

FIVE

The following morning, Caleb found himself outside two offices, each proclaiming that they were the premises of lawyers. They were in fact the two offices pointed out by the deputy the previous day. He pushed open the door of the one which bore the name JAMES CLAYTON and which did not appear to have anybody waiting. He was immediately met by the stern, questioning gaze of a rather school-ma'amish, elderly woman. It was difficult to tell if this was her normal manner or if she disapproved of black people even daring to enter the office.

'Yes?' she demanded abruptly.

'Good morning, ma'am,' greeted Caleb, rising to the challenge she presented and putting on his best smile. He raised his hat and smiled at her again. 'I am the Reverend Caleb Black—'

'Mr Clayton does not make a habit of making donations to any churches other than his own,' she sniffed airily.

'And very wise too,' said Caleb, again smiling broadly. 'However, I am not here to solicit funds, I do have business which may require the assistance of a lawyer.'

He had long since learned that winning over women such as this one, who seemed to protect their employers as if they were mother hens, was far more important than winning over the actual employer. She looked at him sharply as if questioning what legal business *any* negro could possibly have.

'Mr Clayton is also very busy. He does not see anyone without an appointment.' she said. 'Would you be kind enough to tell me exactly what it is you wish to see him about?'

'Certainly, ma'am,' said Caleb with a broad smile. 'I would like to arrange the transfer of a considerable amount of money to an address back East. It belongs – or rather used to belong – to an old prospector. He unfortunately died, of natural causes I might add, and I would like to ensure that his widow gets his money.'

This explanation appeared to have the effect of making her even more suspicious. She looked at him hard and meaningfully.

'Does this . . . er . . . widow know about this money?' she asked.

'I shouldn't think so for one moment,' said Caleb. 'He only died a couple of days ago.'

'I see,' she said. 'I take it it was you who found him?' Caleb nodded. 'And you found this money and somehow discovered that he has a widow and where she lives. Most strange, most strange.' She looked hard at him again. 'And you want to ensure that she gets this money?' Again Caleb nodded. 'Most unusual,' she continued. 'I have lived out here all my life and I must confess that this is the first time I have ever heard of anyone doing what you propose. Normally if anyone finds money in such a way, they take it for themselves.'

'I must confess that even I find the prospect of keeping it for myself very tempting,' admitted Caleb. 'It is a considerable amount. However, I am a man of God and I do hold certain principles very dear. One of them is that I never steal and keeping this money would, in my view, be stealing. It most certainly does not belong to me.'

She looked him up and down and smiled slightly. 'Most unusual,' she said again. 'Most unusual and, I must say, most refreshing. However, I think consulting a lawyer is an unnecessary expense on your part. I have been in this business long enough to have learned a few things. Since it appears to be a simple matter of transferring funds from one part of the country to another, I see no need for a lawyer. This kind of thing is best dealt with by one of the banks. The bank will have to deal with it anyway. You could save yourself a lot of time and expense by dealing directly with the bank.'

At that moment an inner door opened and a tall, thin, well-dressed man appeared. He scowled briefly at the woman.

'Now don't be too hasty, Mrs Fraser,' he said, smiling at Caleb. 'I happened to overhear your conversation. As chance would have it, I do have a few minutes to spare before my next appointment. Please, er . . . Reverend did you say . . . ?' Caleb nodded as the lawyer cocked his head to one side questioningly. 'Step into my office.' He stood aside and allowed Caleb to enter the office. 'I think we are due for some rain later in the day,' continued Clayton. 'It nearly always rains when the wind is from the west at this time of year. Please, sit down.' Both men sat down and once again the lawyer smiled at Caleb as he leaned on his elbows, raised his hands and placed his fingertips carefully together. 'A considerable amount of money, did I hear you say, and discovered on the body of a prospector?'

Very occasionally Caleb met a man in whom, for no obvious reason, his mistrust rose to the fore immediately and whom he could have punched in the face and thoroughly enjoyed doing so without even knowing anything about the man. When it had happened before, on each occasion Caleb had been proved right in not trusting the man. Apart from the advice given by Mrs Fraser being good advice in his estimation, simply meeting James Clayton had already decided him not to entrust the lawyer with his business.

'I do believe that your . . . er . . . Mrs Fraser has given me the best information,' said Caleb, making to stand up. 'I should have known better than to consult a lawyer in the first place. It is hardly a lawyer's business. It is nothing more than a simple matter of transferring funds to an address in the Eastern states.'

'Ah, yes,' intoned the lawyer. 'An apparently straightforward and seemingly simple matter. Would that things were always as simple as that. Unfortunately they very rarely are.'

'I don't see why not,' said Caleb, sitting down again, briefly prepared to listen to what the lawyer might have to say. 'I have some money which belonged to a third party who is now dead – the prospector. I wish to ensure that his widow gets that money, that is all.'

'Provenance!' declared the lawyer. 'You need to establish, in law, that in the first instance the money did indeed legally belong to the unfortunate deceased and you may also need to prove that he is dead. In the second instance it must be established that the lady whom you claim to be his widow is indeed his widow and therefore entitled to receive it. How much money are we talking about . . . er . . . Reverend? In my experience there are very few prospectors who manage to acquire any real wealth.'

'I don't know for certain,' said Caleb. 'Perhaps thirty thousand dollars.'

He immediately regretted giving the lawyer that information. What Clayton had said sounded almost too plausible somehow. At the same time he knew enough about lawyers to know that some of that profession could make even the simple act of wiping one's nose sound difficult enough to have to enlist their services.

'Do you have difficulty counting?' asked the lawyer. 'I fully understand if you do. It is certainly not at all unusual and there is no great shame. There are a great many white men who are illiterate and I have found that most negroes, through no fault of their own, you understand, can neither read nor write . . .'

Caleb stood up sharply and gazed down at James Clayton, knowing that what he said was largely correct. Nevertheless, he felt rather offended.

'Then it would seem that I am an exception to your rule, Mr Clayton,' he snapped. 'I can read and write as well as any man, including you. I had a good education and I can even understand most legal documents and language. I most certainly can count, I am an ordained minister and I was a lieutenant in the army. I think we had better bring this matter to a close. I thank you for your time, Mr Clayton but I do believe that your Mrs Fraser gave me the best advice. I shall go and see one of the banks. I am quite certain that they will not require the proofs you claim. Apart from the dead body of an old prospector at present with an undertaker, I am in no position to provide proof. I have a lot of gold which belonged to this prospector and I have an address which appears to be that of his wife, that is all.'

'Please, Reverend.' The lawyer grinned, apparently completely untroubled by Caleb's outburst. 'I can see that you are indeed an educated man, I meant no insult. I suggest that we discuss the matter—'

'Sorry, Mr Clayton,' said Caleb. 'My mother always warned me not to trust lawyers and I think she was probably right. Good day to you, sir.'

He turned sharply and left the office, giving Mrs Fraser a big smile as he did so. She appeared rather bewildered and even more so when Clayton roared at her to join him in his office.

There was a bank a few yards along the street but there were, according to one of the clerks, at least ten other people waiting to see the president. Caleb explained his business to the clerk who said that although it appeared to be straightforward and routine business, he did not have the authority to act and that Caleb would indeed need to see the president of the bank. He offered to make Caleb an appointment for the following day.

'Gold, you say,' said the clerk. 'I *can* tell you that we

cannot arrange the transfer of gold. At least not in the normal run of business. It would need to be converted into cash and then we can arrange for a transfer of funds by telegraph. It is quite simple and perfectly safe and legal and is most certainly the most efficient way of doing business. I suggest that you sell the gold. There is a government assay office further down the street.'

'A good idea,' admitted Caleb. 'OK, I'll see whoever I have to see tomorrow morning. I take it you do have offices back East.'

'Indeed we do,' beamed the clerk. 'We are a branch of one of the three largest banks in the whole of the United States of America. In fact we can also arrange business as far away as Europe if needs be.'

'Back East will do fine,' said Caleb with a broad grin.

Caleb located the assay office easily enough, even if it was a single office considerably smaller and narrower than all the other stores and offices and quite easy to miss. There was a small but very sturdy counter from wall to wall, complete with stout metal grille and an impressively large and very solid-looking safe at the rear which occupied at least half the room. The clerk behind the desk looked impassive as Caleb placed the pouches of gold on the counter.

'You have been busy,' said the clerk as he poured the contents of the first pouch into a brass dish, examined it, tested it, weighed it and wrote down some figures. 'You don't look like a prospector, but you never can tell these days.'

'I'm not,' admitted Caleb. Although there seemed to be no need, he explained to the clerk what had happened. The clerk, in the meantime, weighed and tested the remaining pouches.

'And she is going to be quite a rich woman,' said the clerk when both he and Caleb finished at about the same time. 'People come in here with perhaps two or three thousand dollars' worth of gold at most with most of them only having a few hundred dollars' worth. I even had two men in yesterday with forty-five dollars' worth. How they came by it I do not know, they certainly did not appear to be prospectors, but they had a pouch exactly the same as these. I'd say they either stole it or won it somehow. It's been a long time since I've seen this much gold all at once and all of it the best quality. In fact, Reverend, I do not have enough money in the safe to pay you out. This little lot comes to more than thirty-two thousand dollars. I can get more cash and if you can come back this afternoon there will be no problem.'

'I would feel a lot safer if I could leave this here,' said Caleb. 'From what I've seen of Morgan City so far I don't feel safe carrying it about.'

'That's no problem,' said the clerk, 'and I agree with you, Morgan City is hardly the place to advertise the fact that you have a lot of money. Men have had their throats slit for just a few cents before now.'

'These two men who sold that gold yesterday,' said Caleb. 'They weren't a negro and a white man were they?'

'Indeed they were,' confirmed the clerk. 'It is not too unusual to see such pairings but again uncommon enough to be noticed. I seem to remember the white man using the name Leroy when he talked to the black man.'

'Billy McGovern and Leroy Smith,' said Caleb with a satisfied grin. 'At least I know they're here. I suppose it's too much to expect that you might know where they are staying?'

'Unfortunately I left my crystal ball at home,' said the clerk with a laugh. 'I am beginning to suspect that there is rather more to you than meets the eye ... Reverend.'

'Oh, I *am* a minister,' confirmed Caleb. 'Fortunately or unfortunately I do not have a regular parish and do not want one. That means I needs must supplement my income in one way or another.'

'It seems to me that thirty-two thousand dollars is a pretty good way to supplement anyone's income,' said the clerk.

'But that would be stealing,' said Caleb. 'Thank you for your assistance. I shall return this afternoon. Good day to you.'

Years of observation, of noting that which appeared out of place, had honed Caleb's senses. He did not miss the fact that two men on the opposite side of the street seemed to be taking great pains to hide the fact that they had been watching him. Immediately his mind sifted through the possibilities.

He could not recall seeing any strange characters in the bank and certainly not either of these men. Neither had they been in the assay office; apart from its being far too small to allow more than a couple of people in at any one time, he had been alone. He remembered the lawyer, James Clayton and, rightly or wrongly on what little evidence there was so far, he strongly suspected that James Clayton might well have something to do with the two men now showing obvious interest.

He resolved to discover more about the two men. They did not appear to be what he might term *outlaws* since neither wore a gun and they were certainly not big enough to rely on brute force. In fact in most ways they appeared to be perfectly normal, law-abiding citizens. He deliberately crossed the street and headed straight for them.

This obviously caused some confusion and seemed to frighten them both as they suddenly walked very quickly along the boardwalk away from Caleb. He smiled to himself and decided to go and see the sheriff. He needed to confirm that it would be in order to arrange for the burial of the prospector in any case.

It seemed that the sheriff had been informed of Caleb's arrival and of the body. In fact and unbeknown to Caleb, the sheriff had arranged for a doctor to examine the body.

'Doctor reckons it was a heart attack,' said the sheriff. 'I guess that lets everybody off the hook. I hear you found a lot of gold on him an' are lookin' to send it back East to his wife.'

'Indeed, so,' confirmed Caleb. 'I am at the moment trying to arrange for the transfer of that gold, or rather money. I am selling it to the assay office.'

The sheriff laughed and slapped the table with the flat of his hand.

'Now I heard everythin',' he said, laughing again. 'I don't know how much is involved, but you're the first man I ever met what don't want to keep money what comes that easy. You plainly ain't from round these parts, Reverend. There ain't a man in Morgan City, exceptin', it seems, you, whose one aim in life is not to chase an' find as much money as possible an' most wouldn't care a damn how they got it.'

'Including you?' asked Caleb.

'Includin' me,' confirmed the sheriff with another laugh. 'Only thing is I wouldn't murder a man or set out to rob him just to get it. Man, I'll tell you straight though, if I was to find enough gold or money on a dead man, I'd make sure nobody knew about it, then I'd take it an' get the hell out of here as fast as I could.'

'Then that might explain why two men were following me,' said Caleb. 'They have somehow discovered that there is a good chance I have something over thirty thousand dollars in my possession.'

'Thirty thou . . .' whistled the sheriff. 'You got yourself thirty thousand dollars an' you want to give it away? I think maybe I'd better get the doc to look at your head. You must've taken one hell of a knock recently. He'd probably certify you insane. Are you serious?' Caleb nodded. 'And are you serious about sendin' it back to his widow?' Again Caleb nodded. 'My deputy said you wanted to send money but I wasn't so sure I believed him.'

'I realize it must seem very strange,' said Caleb. 'Perhaps it might help if I explain who I am. On the other hand it will probably confuse you even more.' He went on to explain that he was a bounty hunter and how and why he was now in Morgan City.

'You're right about one thing,' said the sheriff. 'You got me even more confused. Bounty hunters is lookin' for money, not to give it away. OK, you is plainly quite mad but I accept what you say even if I do find it difficult to understand. You reckon this Billy McGovern an' Leroy Smith are right here in Morgan City?'

'Certain of it,' said Caleb. 'US Marshal Sam Warlock is just as certain and he says he's going to find them before I do.'

'If that's what he says, then that's what he'll do,' said the sheriff. 'If nothin' else Sam Warlock is very single minded when it comes to money. He sure don't give it away, that's for certain.'

'I am also quite convinced that those two men were told to follow me by one of your lawyers, James Clayton, who has an office right opposite.'

'Now that does make sense,' said the sheriff. 'There's strong rumour that Clayton has been helpin' himself to clients' money an' I do believe there's some kind of investigator due to look into his business dealin's.'

'And thirty thousand would probably put things right,' said Caleb. 'OK, Sheriff, I'll keep an eye open from now on. I have your permission to go ahead and arrange the funeral then?'

The sheriff nodded. 'There's the town cemetery or there's a few churches, but they cost more. The town cemetery has a steady trade every day. In fact they dig graves without known' if they have customers or not. Saves time they reckon. Just take your old man along an' they'll take him providin' Saul Bannon gives the OK.'

'Just one thing,' said Caleb. 'I have not as yet got that money, the assay office didn't have enough to pay me and I don't have the gold either, that is safely locked away.'

'Why tell me?' asked the sheriff.

'Just in case you had any ideas,' said Caleb, leaving the office.

He considered tackling Clayton about the two men but decided against it. He had no proof that he had sent them. He still had quite some time before he needed to be back at the assay office. He went to the undertaker to arrange and pay for the funeral of the old man. He would conduct the rites himself.

'Am I glad to see you,' muttered the undertaker. 'That old man you brought in is beginning to make his presence known.'

'Everything would appear to be in order,' said Caleb. 'I have the sheriff's permission to bury him.'

'I could've told you that,' said the undertaker. 'The doctor examined him this morning and the sheriff said it was OK to go ahead. Do you want a religious ceremony? Not that there'll be anyone else there. I can arrange for a minister and professional mourners if that's what you want.'

'I am an ordained minister,' said Caleb. 'I require no mourners, professional or otherwise. I shall conduct any service. I gave you twenty dollars. Now by my reckoning it will probably cost a dollar for the grave digger, maybe a dollar to the city council for the grave and perhaps two dollars for your services. I'll be fair and say that five dollars will cover it all. That means you owe me fifteen dollars.'

'Just about right,' muttered the undertaker, plainly disappointed that Caleb had remembered. He grudgingly took fifteen dollars from his wallet and handed it to Caleb. 'Shall we say four o'clock this afternoon?'

'Shall we say right now?' suggested Caleb. 'This after-noon is not at all convenient. I hear that there's always graves available in the town cemetery and I have no idea what the old man's religion was.'

Very grudgingly, Saul Bannon agreed to transport the body to the town cemetery. However he refused to provide anything but the most basic of services. This comprised a rough, simple coffin and buckboard pulled by a mule to carry it to the cemetery. The only other concession was that the mule had a plume of black feathers on its head. Black top hat and black tail-coat were obviously part of the undertaker's normal dress.

The city cemetery proved to be quite some distance away, about two miles according to Caleb's reckoning. Even then it was well out of sight in a large, wooded hollow. As the sheriff had predicted, there were several graves available and after a few words between the undertaker and two grave-diggers, some cash was exchanged and the buckboard led to a plot at the rear of the cemetery.

Ropes were passed round the coffin, it was lowered unceremoniously into the hole and the ropes pulled away. Neither of the grave-diggers bothered to talk to Caleb and as soon as the coffin was in the grave, they started to fill it in. Caleb smiled to himself but did not object. There seemed little point. He did, however, stand quietly over the grave as it was being filled, his head bowed in silent prayer.

'Do you want a ride back to town?' asked Saul Bannon eventually.

Caleb looked about, smiled slightly and shook his head.

'Thank you, my friend, but no,' he said. 'I have time to waste and the walk back will probably do me good.'

'Suit yourself,' said the undertaker. 'It's been nice doing business with you.'

The undertaker had hardly left the cemetery when the two grave-diggers also suddenly disappeared. Caleb never actually saw where they went, but as he looked about, it was plain that the cemetery was now deserted. Or was it? He had the distinct feeling that something was about to happen.

Two men suddenly appeared. One to his left and the other to his right. They were the same men who had been watching him earlier that day. The difference this time was that they were both armed. They advanced silently at first but their intention was quite plain. Suddenly there was a voice to his right.

'Hand over that gold and you just might live,' said the voice.

'No deal, Mr Clayton,' replied Caleb.

'How do you know who I am?' demanded the voice.

'I never forget a voice,' said Caleb. 'I guessed it was you who set these two on to me this morning. I told the sheriff about it. He seems to think that you are shortly about to be investigated for helping yourself to clients' money. He knows about the gold so if you kill me it won't be too hard to put things together.'

'But he'll need to prove it,' said Clayton, stepping from behind a tree. In the meantime the two men had stopped about ten feet away from Caleb and appeared to be awaiting further instructions. 'It's a good system we have in this cemetery,' continued Clayton. 'There's so many bodies in a week for one reason or another, there's always empty graves. Nobody will notice if one has been filled in and I doubt if anyone will look too hard for you. Not even the sheriff. Now, *Reverend*, the gold. I do know you haven't been able to sell it to the assay office as yet and you haven't handed it over to one of the banks.'

'Perhaps not, Clayton,' said Caleb, 'but I don't have it on me. Search me if you don't believe me.'

'Search him!' barked Clayton to the men. 'Strip him bare, but find that gold.'

The two men advanced and, almost casually, Caleb pretended to remove his coat. Quite suddenly both men were very briefly facing Caleb's two guns with Caleb not prepared to risk being shot. His guns roared out and the two men fell to the ground. A single shot from one of their guns thudded harmlessly into a nearby tree.

'I said I didn't have it,' said Caleb, turning on a now very frightened James Clayton. 'I don't tell lies, Mr Clayton. I think the sheriff might like to have a word with you.'

'I heard more'n enough,' said the sheriff as he stepped into view. 'I saw all three of them follow you so I followed them. Easy it was. I think attempted murder will do for a start, Mr Clayton.'

SIX

Neither of the would-be killers was dead, Caleb had not intended to kill them. If he had meant to, they would have been. The one had taken a bullet in his left shoulder, which appeared to have done some considerable damage to the joint. The man was obviously in great pain and could not move his arm. The other man was perhaps more fortunate in that he had nothing more than a messy-looking flesh wound in his right side and below his ribs.

James Clayton's concern for the men was almost nil, he seemed to sneer as he looked at them. However, his concern for himself, although not injured, was paramount as he attempted to distance himself from the injured men. After a few moments' silence on his part, the lawyer managed to find his voice. He loudly claimed they were *not* acting on his authority.

He also protested very loudly at being arrested; insisting again that he had not authorized anything and that in any case the evidence would never stand up in court. He forcefully reminded the sheriff as to who exactly he was and of the various official positions he held. These included being a member of the city council and –

again stressed very strongly and with an obvious element of threat – that he was the chairman of the committee which oversaw the sheriff's office and paid his salary. He said that he was prepared to overlook the incident providing he was allowed to go free immediately and the whole affair forgotten. If not, he promised that the consequence would be the sheriff losing his job.

Quite obviously the sheriff had heard all the threats before and appeared completely unimpressed. He simply smiled, invited the lawyer to do whatever he saw fit, insisted that he was still under arrest, and suggested that he, James Clayton, should find himself a good lawyer.

By this time, realizing that Clayton was attempting to put all the blame on them, both men were insisting that the lawyer had hired them to steal the gold from Caleb and even kill him if it should prove necessary. More important, they also claimed that Clayton hired them on a regular basis to perform such tasks. One of them named two people who had been murdered by them on Clayton's orders. Clayton, of course, protested very loudly that it was all a pack of lies. The sheriff simply smiled and told Calyton that he would be able to present his case to a jury in due time.

On this occasion Caleb did not refuse the ride back to town, even though it did mean riding up with one of the two injured men. All three men were locked in the city jail, a large extension of the building which housed the sheriff's office and the court rooms. Caleb was a little surprised to discover that it had twenty cells and required five full-time jailers.

Business was obviously quite brisk since seven of the cells were already occupied. Four men were charged with the fairly petty and routine crimes of robbing other men, along with a prostitute charged with robbing one of her clients. Another man was charged with unlawful shooting and wounding and the other one with actual murder in that he had slit a man's throat.

A doctor was sent for to examine the injured men but Caleb did not hang around. He felt he had more important matters to attend to – the locating and arrest of Billy McGovern and Leroy Smith before Marshal Sam Warlock had a chance to find them.

With no plan in mind except keeping his eyes open, Caleb eventually found himself wandering along one of the less desirable side-streets, one which had its fair share of unsavoury-looking characters, all idly passing the time and hoping for a few handouts from people such as Caleb. Caleb had no difficulty in refusing their requests.

All seemed to recognize him for a preacher and apart from mainly silent begging, most ignored him. A few eyed him very warily and one or two even seemed to be considering him as a potential victim to rob. In fact it was plain that one particular character, a black man, intended just that. Caleb knew that the man was following him.

He followed Caleb along the street for about thirty yards before suddenly disappearing down a narrow alleyway. Caleb, however was not fooled, he had been expecting something and, as he approached another alley, his would-be attacker suddenly appeared in front of him. The attacker had no time to say a single word, suddenly finding himself looking down the barrel of one of Caleb's Colts and with Caleb's other hand tightly round his throat. Caleb had very large, powerful hands.

'Can I be of assistance, my son?' asked Caleb very quietly and with a broad grin. He squeezed the man's throat tightly, making him choke. 'I can assure you that this particular preacher has no qualms about killing anyone. I compare myself with the sheep-farmer who kills wolves and foxes to protect his flock. I do the same for my flock. I kill or capture vermin all the time. I don't want to kill you, but if necessary I shall.'

The man choked and raised his hands slightly, revealing that he was armed only with a fairly small knife. He made no attempt to use it.

'I . . . I ain't got no gun,' faltered the man. 'I had to sell mine 'cos I needed the money. Don't kill me, all I need is enough money for a bite of food.'

'For drink, you mean,' said Caleb. 'What's your name?'

'Josh, Josh Brown,' said the man.

'Brown? Yes, that figures,' said Caleb. 'Well now, Mr Brown,' he continued, easing his grip on the man's neck. 'Perhaps you are just the man who could help me. In fact you are probably ideal for the job. You are just the kind of evil-smelling, low-life who can hear things and get into places where the rats congregate and be unnoticed. Places where I would find it impossible to go even though I am a black man.'

Brown nodded eagerly.

'I'm glad you agree,' continued Caleb. 'I'm looking for two men. One is a white man named Billy

McGovern and the other is his partner, a negro like us who is called Leroy Smith. Just as I don't believe your real name is Brown, I don't believe Smith is his real name, but it will do, everybody knows him by that name. You can earn yourself a few dollars by finding them for me. I could be quite generous if you were to succeed.'

'Sure thing, Mr . . . er . . . Reveren',' Brown nodded eagerly. 'I had you figured for a preacher as soon as I saw you, but I didn't reckon on you havin' a gun. Preachers don't usually carry guns. Yes, sir, if anyone can find anyone in this hell-hole it's Josh Brown. What they done, run off with the collection plate?' He laughed weakly at his imagined joke.

'Something like that,' said Caleb, releasing his grip on Josh's throat. 'It's nothing that need concern you. All you need to do is find them and tell me where they are.'

'That all?' asked Brown, rather surprised. 'You don't want either of 'em worked over or nothin'? I can work a man over real good. They'd be ready to admit to anythin' when I gets through with 'em.'

'Just find out where they are and let me know,' said Caleb. 'If you do find them, you can leave a message at the sheriff's office.'

'Sheriff's office?' Brown was plainly alarmed at the prospect. 'No deal, Reveren', I ain't goin' nowheres near no sheriff. Sheriffs an' me ain't exactly on friendly terms. All they ever seem to want to do is lock me up.'

'And I can well understand the reason,' said Caleb. 'Very well, no sheriff's office. I shall be waiting outside the assay office at six o'clock this evening and then again at nine o'clock. Do you know where the assay office is and can you tell the time?'

'I knows the assay office sure 'nough,' said Brown. 'Never did learn to read, write but I can work out what time it is.'

'Perhaps you'd better ask somebody if you are not certain,' said Caleb. 'I'll wait for a time but not too long. In fact it would be as well for you to be there even if you don't have anything to tell me.'

'Sure thing, Reveren', sir,' agreed Brown. 'Just one thing. How much is this goin' to be worth to me? All I got to my name right now is fifteen cents an' fifteen cents might just buy me a small glass of beer.'

'For good information I shall be most generous,' said Caleb. 'I haven't decided on exactly how much, but the right information could buy you enough liquor to keep you drunk for a month.'

Brown licked his lips in anticipation. 'Don't suppose you could see your way clear to lettin' me have a few dollars in advance? I need to go into bars and such places, they're the best places for information but they don't like people askin' questions who can't even afford to buy a beer. You know how it is, Reveren', money talks.'

Caleb did know how it was and was inclined to agree that that made some sort of sense. He took a few bills from his top pocket – which Brown eyed greedily – peeled off two one-dollar notes and held them in front of Brown's now sweating face, his greedy eyes firmly fixed on the money.

'And don't get any ideas about trying to get your hands on the rest of this,' warned Caleb. 'Remember, I kill vermin. I think two dollars should be enough to be going on with. Just remember, you are working for me. No Billy McGovern or Leroy Smith, no more money. Do I make myself clear?'

'Yes, sir, Reveren', sir,' said Brown, suddenly snapping mockingly to attention and saluting Caleb.

'An army man I see,' said Caleb with a wry smile. 'I was a soldier once, a long time ago it seems now. Lieutenant Caleb Black, I was in command of an all-Negro cavalry unit during the war. Who were you with?'

'Corps of Engineers, sir,' replied Brown, relaxing slightly and smiling. 'My name really is Brown, Corporal Joshua Brown, Special Operations Unit. Title sounds good but all it meant was we did all the really dirty an' heavy work. Even so, I wanted to stay in but we was all disbanded when the war ended.'

'Unfortunately that was the fate of a great many of us,' said Caleb. 'Now just remember what I said, Corporal. You find McGovern and Smith and I pay you well. Good luck, Corporal.' Both men saluted each other, not mockingly, there was now a certain respect and sincerity on Brown's part.

Caleb felt more than satisfied with what he had achieved. He had no doubts that his two dollars would soon be used up on drink, but at the same time he felt that he and Josh Brown had reached an understanding.

About half an hour later, Caleb was heading towards his hotel when he saw two men, one plainly white and the other a Negro, slowly walking ahead of him along the boardwalk. There was little doubt in his mind that he had suddenly come across McGovern and Smith.

He removed one of his Colts from his gunbelt and

put the gun in his coat pocket. The reason for this was quite simple; his long coat might have been ideal for hiding the fact that he had two guns and it often suited his purpose to keep one of them out of sight, but it did not allow for a fast draw.

He was now only a few yards behind the two outlaws and it seemed that they had neither seen nor heard him. A few more quick paces and he started to draw the gun in his pocket. . . .

Quite suddenly the comparative silence of the street was shattered as a lone horseman raced from a side street opposite and straight towards them. McGovern and Smith took one look at the approaching rider and suddenly disappeared down an alleyway. The rider fired a couple of shots after them, let out a loud yell and jerked his horse to a halt right in front of Caleb. A broad smile crossed the man's face as he touched the brim of his hat in a mock salute. Marshal Sam Warlock had arrived.

'Evenin', Reverend,' greeted the marshal with another broad grin. 'Enjoyin' your stroll?'

'You just cost me two thousand five hundred dollars,' complained Caleb. 'Those two men who went down the alleyway, they were Billy McGovern and Leroy Smith. I was about to take them in.'

'Sure, I knows that,' replied the marshal with yet another grin. 'I saw what was goin' to happen so I had to do somethin' pretty damned quick.'

'You wanted them to escape!' cried Caleb. 'What the hell for?'

'To make sure you didn't collect no reward money,' said the marshal. 'I thought I made myself pretty darned clear on that, Reverend. Them two is mine. They is in my territory an' I don't allow nobody else, especially bounty huntin' preachers, to pick fruit from my orchard.'

'Wild fruit is there for anyone to pick,' said Caleb. 'It's only stealing when they come from cultivated trees and those two are far from being cultivated.'

The marshal laughed. 'I won't even try an' win a war of words with you, Reverend. Even if you are a negro I knows darned well I'd lose. I mean what I say about them two belong to me though. If you don't forget all about them I could make life very difficult for you.'

This time Caleb laughed. 'Marshal, I have no doubt that you can arrange a lot of things, including my murder if you wanted to. As for making life difficult for me, I doubt you could make it any more difficult than it already is. Take a look at me, Marshal, what do you see? You see a black man, a negro and believe me that's a bad enough hand for any man to be dealt in these parts. No, Marshal, nature doesn't need any assistance from you. I might be an educated negro but that doesn't mean a thing. My skin is still black and that's enough excuse for a good many. I've been spat on, swore at and beaten simply because of the colour of my skin. In fact I think only the Indians might have it worse than a black man. You wouldn't know about things like that though. No white man can ever know what it really feels like. Most think of a negro as closer to animals than human beings and Indians are rated lower still. Do your damndest, Marshal, make life as difficult for me as you can, I still intend to collect that money on McGovern and Smith.'

'A very pretty speech, Reverend,' said the marshal with a grin. 'You're wastin' your time on me though. You don't mean nothin' to me, I'm just one of your bigoted white men who hates blacks an' Indians. You just bear in mind what I just said.'

'And by acting the way you did you might have lost those two permanently,' said Caleb.

'No, sir,' said the marshal. 'I'll find 'em again. There ain't no man can even fart in Morgan City without me knowin' about it if I want to. For instance I knows all about you bringin' in that old prospector an' all his gold. I hear tell it could be as much as fifty thousand dollars. Now that's what I call real money. You don't need the two thousand for McGovern an' Smith.'

'Then your information should also tell you that I am sending that money to the man's widow back East,' replied Caleb.

'Bullshit!' snapped the marshal. 'Sure, I heard you was goin' to wire that money back East an' I can understand that. What I don't believe is that you is sendin' it to the prospector's widow. I reckon you is sendin' it back to your own mother or maybe even your woman. Preachers are allowed women, ain't they? I knows a Catholic priest what has himself a woman an' a couple of kids an' I knows they ain't supposed to. Somethin' about bein' celibate. No sex, that's supposed to mean. Are you celibate, Reverend?'

He did not give Caleb the opportunity to reply as he laughingly urged his horse into a gallop and soon disappeared along the street. For some reason unknown to him, Caleb found himself heading for the sheriff's office.

'Doss-houses or roomin'-houses,' asserted the sheriff in answer to Caleb's question as to where he might find McGovern and Smith. 'Types like that don't go in for luxury. All they need is a doss-house complete with cockroaches, ticks, fleas an' bedbugs an' a rough whore, the rougher the better.'

'That sounds about right,' agreed Caleb. 'What's the difference between a doss-house and a rooming-house?'

'And there was me thinkin' you was a man of the world, Reverend,' said the sheriff with a dry laugh. 'A roomin'-house is just what it says, a house what lets out rooms. They have a bed, a mattress an' maybe a blanket. In a doss-house everybody sleeps in one room an' usually on the floor or maybe on hard, boarded bunks. If you're lucky or pay a bit extra they give you a palliasse but for the most part all you get is old, dirty straw. Roaches, ticks, fleas an' bedbugs come free as part of the deal. Rough whores are usually there for the takin' as well.'

'I thought that might be the case,' said Caleb. 'It's just that they're normally all called rooming-houses elsewhere. OK, so where is the best area to start looking? I've got to start somewhere, I can't afford to just hang about hoping to see them again. I almost struck lucky when I saw them in the street just now, but I didn't reckon on Marshal Warlock being around.'

'That's Warlock,' sighed the sheriff. 'He's never around when I could do with his help but he only has to smell money an' he's there. It ain't often I do need his help, in fact it's normally a lot better when he stays away. I'm sheriff round here, not Warlock. There's nothin' I'd like more than to see somebody get one over on him, but I guess that's somethin' I'll never see.'

'Keep watching,' said Caleb. 'Where is the best place to start looking for McGovern and Smith?'

'Normally I'd say down along River Road,' said the sheriff. 'Only problem with that is that somebody like you would really stand out an' at best all you'd meet is a wall of silence. At worst you could end up in the river with your throat cut, especially if there's even a suspicion that you might have a few dollars in your pockets. We find more dead bodies an' folk beaten up down by River Road than in the rest of Morgan City together. It ain't often we find out who did anythin' an' for the most part we don't even try. Most of 'em are drifters anyway an' nobody don't care about drifters. Even the victims what survive won't normally talk. I'd forget all about lookin' for them if I was you.'

'But you're not me,' replied Caleb. 'Right now, I've got a man to see.'

'Suit yourself,' said the sheriff. 'Tell you what I'll do. I'll get my men to ask around. They can usually find out about things.'

'Thanks, I'd appreciate any help.'

He met Josh Brown outside the assay office. In fact Josh was there before he was. Josh shook his head as Caleb approached.

'Seems like your men have just vanished off the face of the earth,' said Josh. 'I found folk what knew about 'em but suddenly their memories ain't what they used to be. I even bought a couple of 'em a beer but it didn't amount to anythin'. Don't know what your men have done but the word is out that Marshal Sam Warlock is lookin' for 'em as well. In these parts, when Warlock is after somebody that's real bad news for whoever it is and real bad news for anyone what tries to stop Warlock, gets in his way or tries to help whoever he's after.'

'They *are* about,' said Caleb. 'I saw them myself not too long ago. I don't think they've had time to leave town just yet. I know and they know that Warlock is looking for them. I think they'll lie low somewhere until it gets dark and then try to leave. I need to get to them before Warlock does.'

'I guess you knows your own business, Reveren',' said Josh. 'OK, I'll still keep lookin' an' askin' questions if that's what you want. Only thing is I'm goin' need some more money.'

Caleb sighed. He had been expecting just such a request. He did not have any more one-dollar notes so he peeled off a five-dollar bill and handed it to Josh. He also made it plain that there would be no more unless he, Josh, came up with something definite. If Sam Warlock reached either of them before Caleb, the deal was off. He arranged to meet Josh again at nine o' clock.

Even with Josh looking for the two outlaws, Caleb decided to search for them as well but it appeared that Josh's claims about them having disappeared off the face of the earth was correct. Eventually he met up again with Josh who also had nothing to report other than that he had seen Sam Warlock along the notorious River Road just before he met Caleb. He tried to get more money out of Caleb but failed.

Out of little more than idle curiosity, Caleb also decided to go down to River Road. Purely as a precaution, he once again transferred one of his Colts to the pocket of his coat.

Although it was now dark, from what he could see of River Road it did not appear to be any different from most of the other side-roads of Morgan City. The main difference was that there were buildings only along one side. The other side consisted of a slippery, muddy bank down to the water. There were a few dim lights on the opposite bank of the river but apparently little else.

The buildings in River Road provided quite a good if sometimes rather dim light and the bars seemed to be well patronized, very noisy and certainly very smelly. Caleb did look inside one or two of them, but he did not actually go inside. From what he could see they were certainly not places where a lone man would be safe, especially someone such as he who gave the impression of having money.

He did manage to walk the full length of the road without anyone attempting to rob him. Inevitably he was approached by both beggars and prostitutes, some white, some black, one or two who were obviously Indian and even one Chinese woman. In the main the beggars simply grumbled in drunken incoherence and went on their way but most of the whores seemed to take his refusal of their services as personal and swore loudly at him.

Having reached what was plainly the end of River Road, Caleb decided that the only way he was going to find his way back to his hotel was to return along the road. It was not a prospect he relished but he knew it might take him far too long going another way.

On this occasion his journey was not quite so smooth. At the second bar a fight between five or six men suddenly spilled out on to the street directly in front of him and he was forced to hold back whilst the men sorted themselves out. The fight eventually appeared to end when two of the men were thrown down the muddy bank and into the river. One managed to pull himself out but the other seemed to be unconcious and lay face down in the muddy water.

Caleb's impulse was to clamber down the bank and pull the man clear but two of the others, now standing triumphantly at the top of the bank simply laughed, saw Caleb and warned him to leave the man alone. Caleb choked back his impulse to draw his gun and save the man. He continued along the street. He had no doubt that the sheriff would have another dead body on his hands in the morning.

There were two more fights, both of which he managed to get round and it was just as he negotiated the second of these that he saw them. There was no doubt about it, Billy McGovern and Leroy Smith were a few yards ahead of him. His hand automatically slipped to the gun in his pocket.

However, before he had a chance to get to the two men, a third figure suddenly leapt out of the shadows and stood between Caleb and the outlaws, his back towards Caleb. The figure raised his gun . . . .

Caleb did not attempt to shoot either Sam Warlock or the two outlaws. Instead his two shots were fired aimlessly into the air. However, it was enough to enable McGovern and Smith to disappear into the blackness.

Sam Warlock turned on Caleb, his eyes blazing hatred, lit up by dim light from a nearby saloon, his gun aimed at Caleb's chest. Caleb's gun was also aimed at Warlock. There was an obvious stalemate. It was then that Caleb realized that River Road had suddenly become very quiet.

'You first or me?' suggested Caleb as both men stared along the barrels of their guns at each other. 'I guess that makes us even,' he continued. 'Now we've both lost two thousand five hundred dollars.'

SEVEN

'I ought to kill you right here an' now, you bastard,'
grated Sam Warlock. 'I told you to keep the hell out of
my business an' I meant what I said. I'm a powerful
man in these parts an' when I say somethin' folk listen
an' obey. I'm givin' you twenty-four hours to get your
black ass out of Morgan City, Mr Preacher Man. If I so
much as smell you around after that, I'll kill you. I ain't
got no worries about killin' a minister of the church –
any church. None of 'em mean a darned thing to me.
I'm earmarked for the other place anyhow, I reckon, if
there is anywhere after this life. You've got twenty-four
hours to save your black hide. Do I make myself plain?'

'I don't think you could have put it more succinctly,'
said Caleb. 'Most generous of you. Twenty-four hours
should be enough time for me to complete *my* business.
Just remember that that business includes collecting
the rewards on McGovern and Smith.'

'I already told you, that ain't part of the deal,'
warned the marshal. 'I don't make idle threats. I'll kill
you an' don't think anybody would do anythin' about it
either. Ain't nobody in this town got the guts to do
anythin' except make disapprovin' cluckin' noises. In

any case most'd slit your throat for a dollar, preacher or not. In a way I've got to admire you, you're the first Negro ever to stand up to me but I'll make sure you're the last. In fact I reckon you're the first man of any colour to stand your ground includin' all the holier-than-thou preachers. Won't make no difference though, I'll still kill you an' think nothin' of it. The sheriff thinks he runs this town but I know who really runs it an' it ain't him. Now get the hell out of my sight before I change my mind an' kill you right now.'

Both men very slowly lowered their guns and equally slowly replaced them in their respective holsters. At the same time their eyes never left each other's faces, each expecting the other to try and do something. Neither did and Caleb slowly walked past the marshal, smiling and raising his hat as he did so.

Strangely, or perhaps not since Sam Warlock was involved, there was nobody to be either seen or heard in River Road. The nearby bars were now silent although Caleb was well aware that countless numbers of eyes were straining the darkness to see what was going to happen next. Quite plainly nobody was prepared to chance becoming involved with Sam Warlock.

Caleb could feel the marshal's eyes boring into the back of his head and would not have been too surprised had Warlock tried to shoot him. However, he was ready for any of the telltale signs of a gun being drawn or cocked. There were no telltale sounds and when Caleb glanced back the marshal was nowhere to be seen. He was not really surprised.

'Now I knows for certain that you is completely

crazy,' a voice suddenly said from a dark doorway. Josh
Brown stepped out into what little light there was. 'I
been around this town for a few years now an' that's the
first time I ever did see anyone take on Sam Warlock an'
live to tell the tale. I did see a couple of fellers take him
on but he killed 'em. He can be mighty fast on the draw
when he needs to be. I didn't hear most of what you
said to each other but it's the first time I ever did see
Warlock back down an' he ain't a man to back down to
nobody usually. If anybody shows any defiance at all he
normally just blasts 'em where they stand. Mind, I could
see you both had the drop on each other so to speak.
It'd've been interestin' to see just who killed who.
Personally, my money would probably have been on
you.'

'And you would probably have lost,' said Caleb with
a dry laugh. 'Now you know that miracles *can* happen
even in such a godless place as Morgan City. It just
needs more people to stand up to him, that's all. He's
just like the rest of us, a human being. He bleeds just
like any other man.'

'That's as maybe, although I ain't too sure about him
bein' human,' agreed Josh. 'Fact is, though, most folk
ain't prepared to take the risk, they is more interested
in stayin' alive than you seem to be. Unless a man's got
a death wish, nobody who knows Warlock would dare
stand up to him. Man, if ever I seen a man with a death
wish though, it was you, Reveren'. I think I did hear the
man say you had twenty-four hours to get your black ass
out of Morgan City. He said that bit loud enough so's
folk could hear. He allus does an' I can tell you he sure
as hell means it. He's bein' mighty generous too. Can't

understand that, it ain't like him at all. He normally gives folk one hour at most. Thing is, it seems to me, you made Warlock back down an' he knows that. He can't allow it either. To be exact, he can't allow other folk to see it. He has to kill you or make sure you run scared. I'd say you'd be very wise to do just what he says an' get your black ass out of here pretty damned quick.'

'With luck, twenty-four hours should be long enough,' said Caleb. 'After that I don't mind looking as though I'm running away from him, it means nothing to me. Until then, you just keep looking for McGovern and Smith and leave me to worry about my black ass.'

'It's goin' to cost you more money,' said Josh. 'I ain't suggestin' this time either, I'm tellin'. I don't know what's so hell-fire important about them two but it seems to me that they must be real important if both you an' Warlock is after 'em. Now I knows I warn't at the front of the line when brains was handed out, no, sir, I was almost last in line. The brain I was given might not be too quick on workin' things out or doin' things like readin' or writin', but even I got to figurin' that there's more'n a few dollars to be made out of this. I also figured that if I do find out where they is, Sam Warlock might be just as keen as you to pay for that information. Now I ain't too much in love with the idea of sellin' out to Warlock but I will if I think it's goin' to be worth it. Yes, sir, this sure seems to be worth a whole lot more'n the odd five dollars, a whole lot more. Let's say we start at fifty dollars for now, I ain't a greedy man. For that you gets first take on anythin' I find out.'

'I suppose you could try selling your information to Warlock,' agreed Caleb. 'I don't think you would get very far though. He'd be more likely to have the information beaten out of you than pay you for it. Then, after he had beaten you to a pulp, you would probably become one of the bodies nobody cares about found floating in the river or face down in the mud in River Road. Go ahead, Mr Brown, try dealing with US Marshal Sam Warlock. You said yourself you don't like having anything to do with the law. What sort of price is on your head? It probably isn't much but I've seen Sam Warlock take a man with only fifty dollars on his head. He isn't fussy. Just remember, officially Marshal Sam Warlock *is* the law, even if he is a law unto himself most of the time.'

It was quite obvious that Josh had not expected such a reaction from Caleb, however, he was not quite beaten.

'OK, OK,' he croaked. 'Seems to me you an' Sam Warlock got somethin' goin' between you. I don't know what it might be an' I ain't all that interested. OK, you is right, I can't trust the marshal. Hows about makin' it twenty dollars?'

Caleb suddenly laughed and slapped Josh on the back.

'You're a trier, I'll give you that, Josh. I'll make it another ten dollars,' he suddenly conceded. He took another bill out of his pocket and handed it to Josh who, very strangely as far as Caleb was concerned, took it but looked doubtfully at it. 'That's a lot of drinking money,' continued Caleb. 'Just make sure you keep to your side of the deal and find me McGovern and Smith.'

'Yes, sir, Reveren', sir,' said Josh. 'Don't you worry

your head none 'bout ol' Josh. I made a deal an' I'll keep to it. It's just that I'd rather have the money in small bills or even coin if you got it. If folk see me handin' ten-dollar notes around they'll know I got a few dollars change an' a man can get himself killed for less than five dollars round here if n he ain't careful.'

Caleb laughed but could see sense in what Josh said. He took the note back and found one five-dollar bill, but nothing smaller. He managed to gather another three dollars and a few cents in loose change from his other pockets. Josh appeared rather more happy with this and arranged to meet Caleb outside the assay office at nine o'clock the following morning.

Caleb was thoughtful for a few moments. Josh had said that he thought something was going on between himself and Sam Warlock and in a way he was quite right. Caleb smiled to himself. This was no longer a case of who was going to collect any reward money, it had become a personal feud between the pair of them. The money, useful as it might be, was no longer the driving force. It seemed that each man had to prove that *he* was the better man.

Josh disappeared down a narrow alleyway and Caleb continued along River Road, eventually finding the street which led back to the sheriff's office. He knew he would feel safer once he was back in the main square.

It was about 400 yards back to the sheriff's office and that along a fairly narrow but apparently relatively quiet street. He transferred one of his Colts back to his coat pocket just in case. However, his precaution was of little use as almost immediately a black shape sprang at him, knocking him to the ground and before he could draw his gun, another shape dropped down beside him, this time with a gun. which dug into the side of his head. Caleb froze and waited.

'On your feet, Reveren',' hissed Leroy Smith. 'Yeah, it's me an' Billy. Surprised to see us, Mr Preacher Man? You shouldn't oughta be should you? Word is that you've been askin' questions about us. We been hearin' other things too. First though, why you askin' questions 'bout us, Reveren'?

'Yeah,' said Billy McGovern. 'There's things been goin' on we can't figure out. Word is that you found a whole heap of gold on that prospector what died right in front of us. Fifty thousand in gold they reckon. Not only that but you followed us earlier then for some reason we ain't been able to figure, Marshal Sam Warlock came between us.'

'That's right,' said Smith. 'Then the same thing happens just now, 'ceptin' this time it was you what came between us an' the marshal. What the hell's goin' on round here, Mr Preacher Man?'

'So many questions,' said Caleb rising to his feet and stepping on to the boardwalk. 'I saved you from Sam Warlock again, didn't I? That's the second time. You should be very grateful.'

'Oh, we are, Reveren',' hissed Leroy Smith. 'Believe me, we are. Only thing is we just don't understand why you should bother. We ain't nothin' to you. Until Gold Poison we only seen you once at Burney an' even then we never took no notice of you. We're outlaws, Reveren', an' you know that. What happened just now an' out at Gold Poison don't explain why you been lookin' for us. We both reckon you owe us some answers.'

'They say you found fifty thousand in gold on that old prospector,' said McGovern. 'Where'd you find all that gold? We couldn't find more'n a few dollars. What the hell you done with it now? It sure ain't in your hotel room, we searched there already.'

'The reason I was looking for you is quite simple,' said Caleb. 'It's true, I did find a lot of gold. It was stitched into his saddle. It wasn't fifty thousand but it was a considerable amount. Strangely enough, I felt a little guilty about keeping it all to myself. After all, the man died in front of you, not me. It was almost like an omen. I was going to share my good fortune with you.'

'Bullshit!' grated McGovern. 'No man, includin' ministers or preachers, is willin'ly goin' to share that amount of money with folk they hardly know. There's gotta be another reason, I just know there is. Why *did* you save us from Warlock back in Gold Poison? That just don't make no sense at all. That was well before you even knew that gold existed so you findin' all that gold on that old man can't have anythin' to do with it. Another thing that don't make sense is no man goes around riskin' his own life for two no-good outlaws like us without some damned good reason. Yeah, we're no-goods an' we know it. Talk, Reveren', or you won't live to enjoy any of that gold.'

Caleb was suddenly aware of a movement behind the two men and he was quite certain that they had not noticed. McGovern was obviously becoming agitated as Caleb remained silent. A shadow slowly crept up behind the outlaws.

'I said talk!' snarled McGovern. 'Talk or die, I don't

much care which.' Suddenly both men froze as the barrels of guns were prodded into the backs of their heads.

'Seems my man don't wanna talk,' hissed Josh Brown. 'Also seems that you two don't know the meanin' of the word *gratitude*. Didn't he just stop Marshal Warlock from either killin' you or runnin' you in? He sure did, saw him with my own two eyes, an' what do you do? You threaten to kill him. Now that ain't nice, no sir, it ain't at all nice.' A hand reached round each man in turn and took their guns. 'Now just let me hear you apologize for what you done, that's the least you can do,' continued Josh. 'Go on, let's hear you say you is sorry.'

Billy McGovern moved very fast; Josh Brown doubled up in pain, the guns he had taken clattering to the decking of the boardwalk and seemingly disappearing. At the same time Caleb leapt forward to grab Leroy Smith, but Smith proved a little too agile. A fist slammed into Caleb's face, there was a brief struggle between McGovern and Brown but the two outlaws were suddenly racing along the street in the direction of River Road. They were quickly swallowed by the darkness. Josh Brown struggled to his feet gasping for breath but with a broad grin across his face. He wiped away some blood oozing from his nose and grinned again.

'I guess you found 'em,' he wheezed. 'Man, I ain't used to this kind of thing. I been livin' the easy life too long. You OK, Reveren'?'

'I ought to be asking you that question,' said Caleb. 'I thank you for your timely intervention, Josh. I'm not at all sure what they would have done had you not arrived.'

'Don't know what's goin' on,' said Josh, 'an' like I said, I don't wanna know, but it sure seems them two ain't friends of yours.' He suddenly laughed and jumped off the boardwalk. 'Guns, they left their guns. . . .' He scrabbled about in the darkness underneath the boardwalk and eventually stood up, grinning with delight and bearing two pistols. 'Two of 'em. That means I can sell one an' keep one. I ain't felt properly dressed since I had to sell my gun.'

'Pardon me for asking,' said Caleb, 'but didn't you have guns just now? What was that you prodded into the backs of their heads?'

Josh laughed, looked about the boardwalk and eventually picked up two pieces of wood, small pieces of branches from a tree.

'Bang, you're dead,' he said, laughing. 'This is all they was, Reveren'. I used 'em before a couple of times when I was robbin' somebody. Nobody don't know no difference between a piece of wood an' a pistol barrel when it's in the back of his head. Leastways nobody ain't prepared to take the chance. They just might be wrong an' if they is wrong . . . Bang! they is dead. Would you know the difference? I don't think you'd take the chance.'

'It strikes me as a very risky thing to do,' said Caleb. 'You could easily have been killed.'

'Worked though, didn't it?' said Josh. 'I guess that means you owe me, Reveren'. Don't want nothin' just now though, but you make sure you got plenty of small notes, no more'n five dollar bills, on you when I sees you tomorrow. Reckon you'll be all right to find your way back to your hotel?'

Caleb indicated that he was.

'Good,' continued Josh. 'I got me a woman gettin' hersel' in a sweat over me. I'm late already. Be seein' you, Reveren'.'

Josh turned a corner and disappeared from view. Caleb stood staring into the darkness for a few moments but eventually smiled to himself and continued along the street. On the way he met the sheriff.

'I heard you just had a run in with Warlock,' said the sheriff. 'I hear he's given you twenty-four hours to get out of Morgan City.'

'He did say something to that effect,' agreed Caleb. 'What happens if I'm not gone by then?'

'Nothin' as far as I'm concerned,' said the sheriff. 'But then I won't do nothin' if you turn up dead somewhere either.'

'If that happens I can assure you I'll be long past caring what anyone does,' said Caleb. 'I'll say this for Morgan City, news travels extremely fast.'

'Sure does,' said the sheriff. 'Especially bad news.'

Caleb reached his hotel without further incident and the remainder of the night passed peacefully. He was awake at first light, shaved in cold water and then spent the first half-hour in an eating-house where he dined on a thick ham and three eggs followed by a strong coffee.

Apart from a few eating-houses, it appeared that normal business in Morgan City kept to rather more leisurely hours than business in other towns. Other businesses, however, started later and did not close until the early hours of the morning. It was about eight o'clock before the first stores were taking down their shutters.

The banks and the assay office kept even more leisurely hours. The assay office opened its doors at 9.00 a.m. and the bank, according to the notice outside, opened to the public at 10.00 a.m. Caleb settled himself outside the assay office.

As expected Josh Brown arrived just before nine o'clock. It seemed obvious that he had not had much sleep the previous night.

'Cost me two dollars for the night,' muttered Josh. 'Sure was worth it though. Best woman I had in many a year. You should get yoursel' a woman sometime, Reveren'.'

'That is something which comes well down my list of priorities,' said Caleb. 'Do you have any news on McGovern and Smith?'

'Not much,' admitted Josh. 'They is in a doss-house in River Road, I knows that. Only trouble is there's six doss-houses along the road an' I don't know which one. I'm still workin' on that. I did find out that they is wanted outlaws each with about two thousand dollars on their heads. I guess you know that though. I also found out that they lost their horses an' saddles an' two rifles in a card-game. Some folk never learn. It just don't pay to play cards except for pennies an' then only with folk you know. I never gamble. Anyhow, now they ain't got no horses nor guns. I sold one of their guns this mornin'. Twenty dollars is all I could get for it. Must've been worth twice that at least. Still, it's better'n nothin'. I still got the other gun. Anyhow, it seems they been tryin' to get the hell out of Morgan City but with no horses an' now no guns, they is stuck.'

'Just like you,' said Caleb.

'Sure, just like me,' admitted Josh. 'I came here over four years ago now, or was it five? Might even be six, I sure as hell can't remember an' it don't matter none. I ain't got me no horse an' saddle either an' don't particularly want either. I never did like ridin' horses. Anyhow, I ain't so sure as I want to leave Morgan City now. I'm a town man, see, an' town men don't have no need for horses, they never go anywhere. Anyhow I hate the wide open country. All that open space scares the hell out of me an' forests are even worse. There's bears an' wolves in forests an' I hear stories about how a man can empty a whole chamber of bullets into a bear an' the bear hardly feels it. When I was a kid I did see a man who'd had his guts ripped out by a single swipe of a bear's claws. No, sir, I'll take my chance in the city any time.'

At that moment the assay office opened and Caleb went inside. Josh disappeared without asking for more money which surprised Caleb somewhat. After a few preliminaries and the signing of a couple of forms, the assay clerk handed Caleb a large bundle of money and invited him to check that it was all there. Caleb assured the clerk that he believed him. The total amount was $32,476. Caleb put the $476 into his inside pocket, that was his. He felt able to justify keeping that amount as legitimate expenses.

He then went across the street to the bank where he had an appointment. He was immediately ushered into the president's office. His business with the bank was

conducted with great efficiency and without any questions or comments, almost as though it was an everyday
occurrence to deal in such large amounts. The president offered Caleb a drink of wine, which he accepted.
He did not drink wine very often but enjoyed it when
he did.

He was told to check with the bank in two days' time
to make certain that the transaction had been
completed. If, for any reason, it had not been, the
money would be refunded to him – less a suitable
handling fee of course.

Remembering that Josh preferred small denomination notes, Caleb ensured that he had fifty dollars in
one-dollar bills and fifty dollars in five-dollar bills. He
was prepared to pay Josh a hundred dollars for his
services so far. The fact that he had probably saved his
life the previous night warranted the hundred dollars
on its own. He was ready to pay even more if necessary.

His business completed, Caleb stepped out on to the
street. He was immediately faced by three men, one of
them being Marshal Sam Warlock. The other two, judg-
ing by the fact that they also wore stars, appeared to be
deputies. These two stared at him with completely
blank expressions on their faces.

Very few men had completely expressionless faces
but these two were apparently so gifted. He had heard
that there were people called the living dead, or
zombies, who lived on some island well off the eastern
coast. They had apparently died but had been brought
back to life by strange rites. He wondered if Warlock
recruited the living dead. His name did, after all, imply
wizardry.

'I guess you ain't got no reason to hang about Morgan City no more,' sneered Warlock. 'I heard you just wired off thirty thousand dollars. Nice work for some. I still don't believe it was sent to the old man's widder though.'

'Then you must also have heard that I have to check in two days' time that the transaction has been completed,' said Caleb. 'I wouldn't need to check if I was sending it to someone I know. That also means that I have to hang about this god-forsaken city for another two days.'

'You've got until midnight tonight,' said Warlock. 'One minute after midnight and you can start crossin' off the minutes 'til you die. By the way, I've found out where Billy McGovern an' Leroy Smith are. They'll be in my hands in the next couple of hours.'

Warlock laughed and nodded his head at the two deputies who obediently followed him along the board-walk. Old men and women were simply forced aside.

Caleb suddenly found Josh at his side.

'He's right about findin' out where them two are,' said Josh. 'I just been talkin' to a friend of mine. Ain't no way you is goin' to get to 'em 'fore he does now.'

'But not before you can,' Caleb suddenly said. 'Do you know where they are right now?'

Josh nodded.

'Then get to them and warn them,' continued Caleb. 'Tell them to get the hell out of Morgan City even if it means they have to walk.'

'Reveren',' sighed Josh. 'I ain't never been so confused in all my life. First you want 'em, now you want 'em to make a run for it. OK, OK, I won't ask why,

112

I probably wouldn't understand. I'll find 'em an' tell 'em.'

'And there'll be a hundred dollars in small bills for you when you get back,' said Caleb. 'I'll meet you here at noon.'

'One hun . . . !' gasped Josh. 'Yes, sir, Reveren' Lieutenant, sir. Just one thing. Keep your eyes open for Warlock's deputies. They always shoot first an' never ask questions.'

'Those I have seen do not appear capable of *any* form of reason,' said Caleb.

Josh shook his head, plainly not understanding.

EIGHT

'It's just a matter of time now,' a voice said at Caleb's shoulder. He turned slightly to see the sheriff. 'They don't stand a chance,' the sheriff continued. 'Once Sam Warlock has made up his mind on somethin' nothin's goin' to turn him away. I've never known him as bad as this before though. Catchin' them two has become more like an obsession with him.'

'I believe his obsession is not with McGovern and Smith,' said Caleb. 'I think you'll find it has more to do with his being obsessed with me.'

'*You!*' exclaimed the sheriff, plainly surprised. 'Why the hell should he be obsessed by you?'

'Because whatever might have passed for a relationship between us has become very personal,' said Caleb.

'Well whatever it is, it sure seems to get him riled up,' said the sheriff, obviously not quite understanding what Caleb was talking about. 'There's nowhere McGovern an' Smith can hide now. With Warlock rampaging about like he is there ain't nobody goin' to risk hidin' them two. As for helpin' them escape, that'd be like committin' sucide if he found out. I hear he's got twenty deputies out lookin'.'

'Suppose they were to make a run for it,' said Caleb. 'Which direction would give them the best chance of escape? Remember they don't have horses or guns. That would appear to mean to me that open, flat country is out.'

'Well due north leads to desert,' said the sheriff. 'Not much between here an' there either, just a few small farms an' them havin' no horses would make it impossible. West is pretty open too. Farm land at first followed by a patch of scrub and then into cattle-ranching country. East is probably their best chance. That's the way the river flows. It's more or less forest for the first ten miles but after that there's plenty of hills, rocks an' gullies an' a couple of canyons where they can hide. The river eventually runs into a big lake at the foot of the mountains. There's plenty of water about too, even away from the river an' there's no shortage of things like rabbits an' deer for food. How the hell they'd catch any without guns is another matter though. There's a few homesteads an' farms, but not too many, so they might get lucky an' be given or even steal some food. They might even be able to steal a couple of mules, but I doubt it. Mules is what most farmers have up there, they're hardier'n horses but more stubborn. There might be plenty of water but there's not much land about fit enough for growin' things. Most of it is rock, scrub an' sagegrass. What few farmers there are breed sheep or goats.'

'And south is the direction from whence they came,' said Caleb. 'South-east that is. I seem to remember that Rockwood is south-west of here. I think we can rule out Rockwood since that's where the state prison is and where Sam Warlock is based. They both know Rockwood, I think they spent time in prison there. I believe we can rule out anywhere connected with Sam Warlock.'

'Then it would seem their best chance is to head east,' said the sheriff. 'If they did time in the prison they probably know the layout of the land from what they were told if nothin' else. Only thing against all that, though, is Sam Warlock himself. Personally I'd say they have a better chance of out-runnin' a bullet than gettin' past Sam Warlock once he's set his mind on somethin'. By now I reckon he'll have every possible way out of Morgan City well and truly sealed off.'

'Unfortunately I fear that you are probably right,' said Caleb.

Even though the two outlaws had not yet been caught, Caleb knew that both his chance of collecting the reward and their chance of escaping the marshal were growing slimmer by the minute. At least if they were caught by the marshal it would mean that he no longer had any reason to remain in Morgan City other than to check that the money had reached the prospector's widow. However, he had no doubt that the money would find its way to its rightful owner eventually and in any event he had not really intended waiting for confirmation. Had he used that pretext to remain it would simply have been to annoy the marshal.

With little else to do, Caleb even tried looking around the streets for the outlaws by himself, but he very quickly discovered that the two zombies who had been with Sam Warlock were now in constant attendance on him, although always at a distance. Again their expressions were apparently completely without emotion and it seemed to Caleb that their eyelids never blinked. He eventually gave up looking, partly because of his attendants and partly because he knew he was wasting his time. He returned to sit outside the bank and wait for Josh. The zombies took up position opposite, outside the assay office. Josh arrived about an hour later.

'Don't tell me,' sighed Caleb. 'Sam Warlock has this town sealed up tighter than a duck's ass, and that's watertight, and he has twenty deputies out looking for them.'

'OK, so I won't tell you,' said Josh. 'Don't know if he has twenty deputies or not, but he sure has a lot of 'em. I did find your men though. I didn't need to tell 'em about Warlock, they was well ahead of me. It seems the entire city knows what's goin' on. Last I saw of 'em they was headin' down to the river. I hung around waitin' to see what happened 'cos some of Warlock's men followed 'em down there. Don't think they knew they was followin' 'em though. Anyhow, the deputies came back after about half an hour without findin' either of 'em. I can tell you this much, neither of 'em came up into town. I'd've heard if they had. They've gotta be hidin' out somewheres 'cos they know they couldn't trust nobody. Somebody'd be sure turn 'em in to Warlock.'

'Which means that they must still be down by the river,' said Caleb. 'You must know the place pretty well by now. Is there anywhere down there they could hide, anywhere at all?'

'Well, gettin' across the bridge is right out, there's

two deputies this end,' said Josh. 'There's a few shacks along the riverbank but I reckon you can forget them, they'd be the first places even a blind man would look. There's a couple of reed-beds an' I suppose they could hide in there but I reckon even Warlock will think of that. Hidin' in the reeds has been tried before. As far as anybody knows it ain't worked yet. No, Reveren', I reckon wherever they is it's only a matter of time now before Sam Warlock sniffs 'em out.'

'That certainly would appear to be the common opinion,' said Caleb with a deep, almost resigned sigh. 'Well, at least we tried. Unfortunately I suppose I shall have to admit defeat. I don't have the resources the marshal has.'

'Talkin' about resources,' said Josh. 'Didn't you say somethin' about one hundred dollars in small bills?'

'Indeed I did, my dear Josh,' said Caleb with a laugh. He pulled a wad of notes from his inside pocket and held it for Josh to see. 'One hundred dollars in fives and ones just as you asked for. Tens and twenties might have been better, they would have been far less bulky and would have been easier to hide.'

Josh glanced around, growled something about showing the whole world, snatched the money and quickly stuffed it down the front of his shirt, saying that a man could never be too careful about who was watching.

'Thanks, Reveren',' he whispered. 'I ain't never had me so much money before. I'll try to make it last a while. Ones an' fives will do me fine. Like I said, it don't do to let folk see you with bigger bills. That way they know you got money.'

'Take my advice,' said Caleb, 'Don't spend it all on women, drink and gambling.'

'Don't spend it all on women, drink an' gamblin' the man says,' said Josh with a loud laugh. 'Tell me just what the hell else is there to spend money on in this or any other town? Gamblin' won't be no problem to me, I ain't never been a gamblin' man. I seen my pa gamble everythin' he ever owned an' me an' my ma were thrown out on to the street. You can guess how my ma had to earn a livin' for us both. No, sir, no gamblin' but I can have me a good time for a week or two with women an' drink an' then it's back to the old ways. That won't bother me none though. I'll enjoy it while I can an' I reckon it sure won't bother you none either, Reveren'. You'll be long gone before I spend it all an' I reckon you won't even remember my name once you is out of here. Ain't no need for you to remember somebody like me.'

'I'm sure there are other things you could do with it,' said Caleb. 'However, it's your business. All I can say is thanks for what you've done for me. At least we tried, didn't we? Anyway, they haven't actually been caught yet, so there is still a slim chance for me.'

'If you say so, Reveren',' agreed Josh. 'I ain't a gamblin' man but I don't see even a professional gambler bettin' against Sam Warlock. Now, maybe you wouldn't mind tellin' me what all this has been about? I can understand the marshal wantin' to catch them two, that's his job an' there is a good price on their heads from all accounts, but just how do you figure in it all? I would've thought that as a man of religion you would've been on the side of law an' order.'

'I am,' assured Caleb.

'Then you got a mighty strange way of showin' it, mighty strange,' sighed Josh. 'How come then, if you is on the side of the law, you stopped Warlock from arrestin' 'em down in River Road? How come you sent me to warn 'em about what was goin' on? Looks to me like your idea of enforcin' the law an' Warlock's idea ain't quite the same. Warlock's way I can understand, but I sure as hell can't understand yours.'

Caleb laughed and agreed that he did owe Josh something of an explanation. He expressed surprise that the grapevine had not come up with the facts, especially as it appeared to be very efficient and remarkably accurate in all other respects. He explained that he was a bounty hunter and that his sole intention in helping the two avoid Sam Warlock outlaws was to ensure that he, The Reverend Caleb Black, and not Marshal Sam Warlock collected the reward money.

'Then like you say, Mr Reveren' Bounty Hunter,' said Josh, 'it looks like you just lost out. You was right about the price on my head, fifty dollars. At least that was what it was when I first came to Morgan City. Don't know if it's still the same. I reckon you could run me in an' find out.'

'Thanks for the offer,' said Caleb, laughing. 'I won't take you up on it though. Now, just because I'm very curious, I'm going down to the river. Why don't you show me the exact place you last saw the outlaws.'

'OK,' agreed Josh. 'Not much to see though, but I ain't got nothin' else to do at the moment.'

They reached the river and Caleb noted that his zombie entourage was still with him. He raised his hat in their direction but any irony was apparently completely lost on them. On the way, Josh indicated the spot where he had last seen McGovern and Smith, which did not help at all.

Caleb had only been down to the river twice before. The first time was when he first came into Morgan City across the bridge. The second time was in the dark when he walked down River Road. He was surprised at just how wide the river was. It appeared to be the best part of seventy yards or so. It also appeared to be quite shallow with reed-beds in the middle of the river.

He could see the bridge about a hundred yards downstream and saw that it was in effect three separate bridges between two islands. He had not noticed this fact on the way in.

There were several shacks built on stilts over the water and a lot of other shacks along the river bank. Caleb had to agree that such hiding-places would be a little too obvious even for the likes of McGovern and Smith to consider using.

About thirty yards downstream he could see a large reed-bed and, more in hope than expectation, he and Josh moved down to gaze into them. There was no reason to think that the outlaws might be hiding there. Two ducks darting in and out of the reeds appeared to indicate that all was normal.

A little further on from the reed-bed Caleb saw what seemed to be a drainage pipe. Closer examination showed that it was made of brick and did indeed appear to be a drainage pipe. There was a steady flow of foul-looking water into the river. He looked back and was most surprised to see that his escort had disappeared.

He checked all round but it seemed that they had most definitely departed.

'That old pipe,' said Caleb, 'they could be inside. It's definitely large enough for a man or even two men to hide inside.'

'Maybe so,' agreed Josh. 'Been tried before though. That's another of them places where Warlock would know about. It looks big enough an' it is. It don't go very deep, maybe ten or twelve feet under the bank at most. It's fed by smaller pipes. All they do is take water under the road an' mostly they is all blocked up now. They ain't been cleaned out for years. I'll go take a look if you like though.'

'No need,' said Caleb 'It was just an idea. You are probably right, it is rather obvious. How many more are there?'

'Three or four big ones like this,' said Josh. 'Whoever designed this town put in a drainage system on account of it bein' built on marsh. Mostly it's all small ditches an' channels, you must've seen 'em in almost every street. In a few places it has to go underground so they put in brick pipes or in some cases wooden or cast-iron ones. Seems to work pretty good as well, Morgan City don't flood like it did once, so they tell me. There's about twenty or thirty small pipes as well, but I don't think a man could get himself inside one of them.' He pointed out two smaller pipes, each dribbling foul-looking water into the river.

One was very small, apparently made of cast-iron and no more than three or four inches in diameter. The other appeared to be between twelve and fifteen inches in diameter and made of brick. Caleb had to agree that even the brick one seemed too small for anyone to hide in.

The arrival of two deputy marshals made it uneccesary for Josh to look inside the large pipe as one of them, obviously acting on orders, duly obliged, going right inside. He also peered inside the fifteen-inch pipe and fired his gun up it just in case there was anyone foolish enough to be inside. However, a few rats suddenly scuttled out, to the apparent horror of the deputy.

It was obvious that the men were not inside the pipe as the deputy scrambled back up the bank, complaining bitterly about the rats, the foul smell and the state of his clothing. He washed his hands in the water before leaving and Caleb wondered if this made any difference at all to their cleanliness.

There were several small rowing-boats and canoes pulled up on to the bank, although it seemed that all the owners had taken the precaution of removing oars and paddles. The thought crossed Caleb's mind that if he were in the position of McGovern and Smith, one good way out of their predicament might well be to escape by water. In fact it appeared to be the most logical way even if it was also one of the most obvious.

He and Josh then walked as far as the bridge where Caleb stood for some time. He was apparently studying the islands on which the bridge was built. Each was surrounded by reeds. If he thought the two outlaws might have hidden themselves on the islands, the fact that a deputy was searching them appeared to rule out that idea unless they were very well hidden by the reeds.

Later that afternoon Caleb was suddenly confronted

by Marshal Sam Warlock. The two zombies had now re-attached themselves to their master. The marshal sneered at Caleb and quite slowly but very deliberately took out his pocket watch and held it for Caleb to see.

'Midnight,' he hissed. 'Just over eight hours.'

'Did you manage to work that out all by yourself?' said Caleb.

'You keep talkin' like that an' you won't see another midnight ever again,' said Warlock. 'My men tell me you was down by the river. What you want down there? Lookin' for your friends, were you?'

'I just thought that since you plainly haven't yet found them I might—'

'You just thought,' interrupted Warlock. 'I reckon you ought to be thinkin' a whole lot harder about what's goin' to happen to you an' maybe even your friend, Josh. OK, so I ain't found 'em yet, but I will, believe me, I will. If you're so fond of thinkin', Reverend, think about what will happen to you if you ain't out of this city by midnight.'

He pushed roughly past Caleb without giving him the chance to respond. Caleb was also quite surprised to see what might even have been a smile on the face of one of the zombies. An hour later he met Josh who, it appeared, had been looking for him. He told Josh of the not-so-veiled threat made by the marshal about him. Josh simply shrugged.

'So what's new?' said Josh. 'Word is Warlock is on the move. I overheard a couple of his deputies talkin' an' it seems they think your two outlaws is goin' to make a run for it tonight. Seems they think they is goin' to try an' steal a boat or canoe an' head off down river when it gets dark. Anyhow, a few of 'em have already gone down river to cut 'em off.'

'Do you know anything about the river?' asked Caleb.

'Not much,' admitted Josh. 'I ain't never had cause to know. Too open for me an' I hear tell there's bears an' wolves down there. That's good enough for me not to go. I also hear tell there's a waterfall or rapids or somethin' about five miles down, but I ain't never seen 'em nor don't want to. I can find out though.'

'Don't bother,' said Caleb. 'If Warlock's men have gone down river it's probably to these rapids or waterfall. I think I'll follow them. It's just about the only chance McGovern and Smith have of escaping and probably the only chance I have of catching them. In the meantime, you just watch out for Warlock. I don't want you getting yourself killed because of me.'

Caleb followed the river, which had now narrowed to no more than forty yards wide and the light was beginning to fade as Caleb approached what he assumed to be either the rapids or the waterfall. As he drew nearer, the noise changed slightly to a deep, constant roar and, having heard such sounds on many occasions, he guessed that it was a waterfall and probably quite a high one at that.

His approach was quite cautious but need not have been. The area was well wooded and he eventually saw three men sitting on rocks just above where the water disappeared. He also located another man a little further upstream who seemed to be scanning the approach. Any noise Caleb might have made was completely drowned out by the crashing water. It seemed obvious that the deputies were not expecting anyone along the trail.

The man upstream raised his hands and called out. It appeared that there were other deputies on the opposite bank. Caleb would have been surprised had there not been.

At that point the land suddenly dropped very steeply. The trail, such as it was, zigzagged down the steep ridge and fortunately Caleb's progress was obscured from view by the many trees, although he was not too worried about being seen. However he eventually reached the base of the waterfall, apparently without anyone knowing. At least he was not challenged in any way and there did not appear to be any deputies about.

The falls were quite high, something over 120 feet, completely sheer, and he estimated that the river at that point had reduced in width to about twenty yards or so. However, where the flow had been fairly fast but calm further up, it now became a raging, frothy torrent. The falls cascaded into a deep pool which was surrounded by large, jagged rocks. The course of the river was also apparently full of submerged rocks against which a man could easily have been fatally dashed. It appeared obvious that McGovern and Smith would have to take to the bank above the falls.

Caleb made his way back to the top of the falls, again apparently without being seen, and then followed the river upstream. Although he was not particularly worried about being seen, he tried not to make his presence obvious. He followed the river for about a mile and noted that there were men posted at regular intervals along the bank. Men he had not noticed on his way down and it seemed they were oblivious to his presence.

He saw three other riders slowly making their way along the river bank. They stopped frequently and called across the river to other men. The riders proved to be Marshal Sam Warlock and his two zombies. Having no desire to meet the marshal or the zombies, Caleb returned to the falls.

He felt that, if possible, he must see what was happening, although the fading light was going to make that very difficult, He eventually took up position overlooking both the river and the falls.

Darkness closed in very quickly and it was not long before he could see very little at all. He waited for about half an hour, when a distant call could be heard. This call was closely followed by a second and then a third and then shooting. He gathered that a canoe had been sighted, which was not unexpected.

Although his eyesight was very good and he had grown accustomed to the light and had quite a clear view up the river, he could not make out anything which might have been a canoe. The shooting and shouting stopped and Caleb wondered if it had been nothing more than itchy fingers and imagination. There was silence for about five minutes.

Quite suddenly and very close by, the shouting started again and several flares were lit. This time there was no mistaking it. The dark shape of a canoe could be plainly seen in the flickering lights from both banks. A voice called out and challenged the occupants of the canoe but there was no response. The order to shoot was given.

This time it seemed that at least ten guns were shooting at the canoe and they were very accurate. Caleb saw the canoe slowly sinking and it eventually keeled over but it was plain that there was nobody inside. Caleb found himself breathing a sigh of relief.

His position high above the river gave Caleb a different perspective on things. He watched the canoe disappear over the edge of the falls and looked back to see if there was any sign of bodies. Had they been shot, it would not take long for the two bodies to float downstream and over the falls. More men with flaming torches appeared on either bank, making it much easier for Caleb to see.

What he did see made him suddenly leave his viewpoint. He was quite certain that he had seen two heads come up for breath in the middle of the river. He might have been wrong, but he was not prepared to take the chance.

They were approaching the falls very fast and it was obvious that there was no possible way for either of them to reach the comparative safety of the banks. Caleb did not wait to see them go over the edge of the falls. It was easier and most certainly much quicker for him to slither down the ridge on his own, leaving his horse.

He soon reached the base of the falls where all he could hear was the roar of water and, in the dark, could see very little.

NINE

At first and somewhat helplessly, Caleb stood looking into the large pool beneath the falls. His heart sank as he realized that the chances of his ever finding either of the two outlaws alive were almost non-existent. What little light there was reflected off the turbulent water, making it appear as though there could have been many heads or bodies floating in it. What he really thought was a body proved to be a tree-trunk, but he did not discover this until he had taken a thorough soaking whilst attempting to reach it.

Then again, after a very short time, he was quite convinced that he *could* see a body floating towards what appeared to be a quieter, shallower backwater behind some rocks. He quickly clambered across, constantly slipping on moss-covered rocks and at one point having to wade waist-deep and then almost falling back into the water as he slipped whilst hauling himself on to a flat rock.

This time he had been right, it was a body and was floating face downward, not a good omen. Once he was able to reach the body he immediately turned it face up and grabbed at the outstretched arms. He eventually succeeded in pulling the body on to another larger, flat rock.

In his time Caleb had learned some rudimentary methods of resuscitation and very quickly turned the body face down, the head to one side and applied his limited knowledge of ridding lungs of water as he pressed hard on the man's back. The body proved to be that of Billy McGovern.

At the same time as he was pumping away, Caleb was looking around for any sign of Leroy Smith but he could see nothing definite. Again, what little light there was created heads and bodies floating everywhere in the water. However, at the moment he had convinced himself that he had located the body of Leroy Smith, Billy McGovern groaned and reminded Caleb that he was Caleb's immediate priority and not Leroy Smith. Alive, the outlaw was worth $1,000. Dead, Caleb was uncertain if he was worth anything at all. If it had been Leroy Smith he had seen, he would, unfortunately, just have to wait.

After a few more minutes of pressing McGovern's back, Caleb's efforts were rewarded when McGovern coughed and spluttered. A few more seconds of pressure was applied before Caleb was satisfied. However, it was quite plain that McGovern was in no condition to respond to anything else. He seemed to be unconscious.

A sudden flash of light at the top of the falls was quickly followed by some voices and then by two or three flaming torches slowly making their way down the ridge. Caleb shook his head, remembering that he was not alone. He realized that Sam Warlock would ignore any claim he, Caleb, might have and take the bounty for himself. At that moment he had no intention of yielding Billy McGovern up to Sam Warlock and he looked about for somewhere to hide the outlaw.

At first it seemed that there was nowhere, but then he thought he saw a hollow in the cliff behind the cascading water. It was a long shot but the only chance he had and it could easily have been nothing more than a shadow. The torches were now rapidly descending the ridge and it would have been impossible for Caleb to get the body deeper into the forest.

He wasted no time; somehow he managed to lift the body on to his shoulders and then stumble over slippery rocks towards the falls. It might have been no more than ten yards but it was with a great sigh of relief that he found there was indeed a hollow behind the falls. It was just large enough to take McGovern and himself. To reach it he had to force his way through the falling water and almost lost his footing and his grip on his precious load.

A few moments later four burning torches arrived and deputies began searching the water around the pool at the base of the falls. Fortunately for him, they seemed to discount his hiding-place although one of them came within about six feet of him but, cursing loudly, was driven back by the force of the falling water. Eventually he heard a familiar voice.

'Ain't no way they could've survived that drop,' announced Marshal Sam Warlock. 'Ain't much use lookin' for their bodies right now either,' he continued. 'They must've been washed down river. We'll never find 'em in the dark. Let's get back to town, we can start lookin' again at first light. Even if one of 'em survived he's sure to have broken a few bones. They ain't goin' very far.'

It appeared that these instructions were met with some approval by the deputies and it also appeared that his horse had not been discovered. However, Caleb held his breath. His horse was still at the top of the ridge, although fairly well hidden but he knew that should it be discovered, Sam Warlock would not give up so easily. After about ten minutes during which time no cries went up about finding his horse, Caleb was forced to assume that they had returned to town.

Billy McGovern was still unconscious, although he was now breathing more or less normally. There were no obvious signs of any other injuries and the lack of blood in his mouth seemed to indicate no major internal problems.

Satisfied that even without apparent injuries he would be in no condition to go very far, Caleb left him where he was and went to fetch his horse. Fifteen minutes later he had slung McGovern across the horse and was searching the river further downstream, although he was not too hopeful. It was very dark and several times he mistook old tree-stumps or roots for the body.

If Smith had been washed on to the riverbank, he was just as likely to be on the opposite side and therefore easily missed. Caleb had already decided to search downstream for about twenty minutes or so, cross the river and search back along the opposite bank.

Luck, however, seemed to be on Caleb's side; after about ten minutes he thought he heard somebody calling. He stopped and listened. He heard it again, except that this time it was not so much a cry for help as somebody in obvious pain, moaning loudly. He tethered his horse and slowly searched the edge of the river. He almost fell over the body which was partly wedged under the exposed roots of a tree, the legs sticking out and partly on the river bank. Had Caleb not heard the moans, he would have given the man up for dead.

Getting the body from underneath the roots proved to be fairly easy and a few minutes later Caleb had pulled him part-way up the bank. At that point Caleb's worst fears seemed confirmed. He gently tapped Leroy Smith's face expecting no reaction. However, there was sudden splutter and Smith's eyes opened but he did not appear to see anything. The eyes closed and once again Caleb tapped his face, this time a little harder.

'That you, Billy?' croaked Smith as his eyes flickered and opened, once again staring unseeingly. 'I guess we fooled 'em?'

'You certainly did,' agreed Caleb.

'Billy!' Smith croaked again. 'That you, Billy?'

'Billy's alive,' said Caleb. 'He'll be fine. Can you stand up?'

'Well I'll be . . .' said Smith with an attempt at a laugh. 'I'd know that voice anywhere, it's been hauntin' me for days now. Hi there, Reveren', never thought I'd be pleased to see you again. I ain't too sure I am now, either. You allus turn up like a bad penny. Trouble ain't never very far behind you. Can I stand up, the man asks? Might as well ask me if I can fly, Reveren'. No, sir, don't reckon I can. I think I busted both my legs. They don't hurt too bad but they feel a funny shape. I think

I took a bullet in my side as well but I reckon I'll survive.'

'It was a crazy thing to do, try to escape that way,' said Caleb. 'You must have known the marshal would be expecting something like that.'

'Didn't seem half as crazy as just hangin' around an' lettin' Warlock get to us,' croaked Smith. 'There was more'n enough folk ready to sell us out to him. Yeah, we guessed he might be there somewhere but we reckoned it was worth the chance. Only trouble was nobody told us about that damned waterfall. What the hell brings you out here, Reveren'? You allus seem to be about. Like I say, just like a bad penny bringin' a load of trouble.'

'I don't think you could be in much more trouble than you are in right now,' said Caleb. 'I was looking for you. I seem to have done nothing else but look for you. You have been very difficult to find.'

'Well, now you found us,' said Smith with a dry laugh. 'Don't know what state Billy's in but I sure ain't in no condition to put up much of a fight an' right now the last thing I'm lookin' for is a fight of any kind. So you've been lookin' for me an' Billy? Yeah we did hear somethin' like that. Well, now you found us, maybe you can answer the one question what's been buggin' the pair of us ever since Gold Poison. Just what the hell do you want with us? We ain't nobody special, we're both outlaws an' we sure ain't got no money. Just what the hell *do* you want?'

'Two thousand five hundred dollars,' replied Caleb.

'Two thous . . .' said Smith. 'What the hell you talkin' about?'

'It's really quite simple,' said Caleb, as he slowly dragged Smith up on to higher and drier ground, causing the man obvious pain and discomfort but he did not complain. 'I am a bounty hunter and you and Billy McGovern are worth two thousand five hundred dollars to me.'

'Yeah, we know what they're offerin' for us,' said Smith. 'Strangely enough I ain't at all surprised. I said to Billy I thought you was a bounty hunter but he wouldn't have it. He said preachers an' bounty hunters didn't go together.'

'Well I can assure you that I am a fully ordained minister of the church and that I am also a bounty hunter,' said Caleb, examining Smith's injuries as best he could in the dim light. He could feel a bone protruding through the flesh in Smith's upper right leg. 'As far as I am concerned the two are quite compatible.'

'If'n I knew what the hell that meant I might agree with you,' said Smith. 'OK, so you is a bounty hunter. Would you mind tellin' me just why you stopped Warlock from arrestin' us an' why Warlock stopped you? It was pretty plain that's what happened between the pair of you.'

'All in good time,' said Caleb as he felt the obvious break in Smith's other leg, this time below the knee. 'Right now we have to get you to a doctor. Your legs are a real mess. The bullet in your side seems to have passed straight through so it shouldn't be any problem.'

'Can't feel much in my side or my legs,' admitted Smith. 'I knows without even tryin' that I can't stand. If you is expectin' me to ride a horse then I reckon you is dreamin'.'

'I'll think of something,' said Caleb. 'First, I have to get you away from the river. It is just possible that the marshal or one of his deputies might come back. I'm sorry for this, but I'm going to have to drag you further up among the trees. You just hang on now, grit your teeth and try not to yell too loud.'

'Right now it don't matter a shit who finds me,' grated Smith as Caleb took hold of his wrists. 'You pull if you want to, I sure can't stop you, an' I'll yell.'

Strangely, Smith did not cry out too loud and when he did, Caleb stopped pulling him. Eventually Caleb found a well-sheltered spot at the foot of a large pine-tree and almost surrounded by a thick bush. He made Smith as comfortable as he could.

'Now you just lie here and wait,' instructed Caleb. 'Billy doesn't seem to be as badly injured as you, although he's still unconscious. I'm taking him back to town and then I shall come back for you. The only way I'm going to be able to move you is on a wagon. You're right, you'll never ride a horse. Don't worry, I'll bring a doctor back with me, he might make you more comfortable. In the meantime just do me a favour. If you do hear anyone, keep quiet.'

'I'll think about it,' agreed Smith.

'Think hard,' advised Caleb. 'If Sam Warlock or his men find you I don't suppose for one moment they are going to give a damn how many bones you've broken or how many others they'd break taking you back. Another reason to keep quiet is because it could be a bear or a wolf and I don't think they will bother too much about your broken bones either. In fact it might make it easier for them to chew on you.'

'OK, OK,' grunted Smith, 'you is probably right about the marshal an' the bears. OK, you got yourself a deal Mr Reveren' Bounty Hunter. I suppose if anybody is goin' to make any money out of me I'd rather it be you than that damned Marshal Sam Warlock. Now get goin' so's you can get back here quick. I'm startin' to hurt real bad an' I can hear a bear comin'.'

'I wouldn't joke about things like that,' said Caleb. 'I saw a man who'd had his arm bitten off by a bear once. Not a pretty sight.'

'Then get the hell out of here an' get back before some big grizzly or a pack of wolves decides I might make a tasty meal,' grated Smith.

With Billy McGovern still unconscious and now tied across the back of his horse, Caleb made fairly swift progress back to Morgan City. He would not have been surprised to come up against some of Sam Warlock's deputies, but he reached the sheriff's office completely unchallenged. Billy McGovern was taken in to a small room at the rear of the office and a doctor was sent for.

Caleb explained what had happened and that he now needed a wagon and a doctor to bring in Leroy Smith. If the sheriff was surprised at the way things had turned out, he certainly did not show it and arranged for the wagon.

Caleb also made certain that everybody, including the doctor who attended Billy McGovern, the sheriff and a deputy were aware that he, the Reverend Caleb Black, was claiming the bounty on both McGovern and Smith.

After examining McGovern and pronouncing that as far as he was concerned there were no obvious injuries other than concussion, the doctor agreed to accompany Caleb and the sheriff to find Leroy Smith. On hearing just what Smith's injuries were, he insisted on first of all returning to his office for some splints. Eventually, with Caleb on his horse and the sheriff and the doctor on the wagon, they set off. Once again Caleb was very surprised that there was no sign of Sam Warlock or any of his deputies.

Eventually they found Leroy Smith, whose condition now appeared to have deteriorated. He seemed a little delirious and confused but he was still conscious, if only just. The doctor spent some time fixing splints to Smith's legs and then strapping the legs together. When he was satisfied, the three of them lifted the body on to the wagon.

They were within sight of Morgan City when three men on horseback suddenly loomed in front of the wagon. One of them ordered them to stop.

'What you got there, Sheriff?' asked Sam Warlock. 'Looks like a body. Been an accident, has there?'

'Somethin' like that,' said the sheriff. 'He's hurt real bad. We've got to get him back so's the doc here can put him right.'

The marshal moved forward, looked at Caleb, sneered and looked down at Leroy Smith.

'Well now, if it ain't Mr Leroy Smith. I been lookin' for you, Mr Smith. Looks like you survived the falls. You're lucky to be alive but maybe you won't think so later.'

'Billy McGovern survived as well,' said Caleb. 'I brought him in earlier. I'm claiming bounty on both these men.'

'Now that don't seem right to me,' said Warlock, once again sneering at Caleb. 'No, sir, it don't seem right at all, not after all the hard work me an' my men put in lookin' for both of 'em. 'Sides, I already warned you, Mr Preacher Man, that nobody don't collect no bounty off nobody in my territory exceptin' me an' I don't make no exceptions for bounty huntin' black preachers either. OK, you can take him back, Sheriff. I'll be along in the mornin' to see the judge an' sign the forms for the bounty. That goes for McGovern as well. I don't care who brought him in.'

The sheriff looked hard at Caleb, plainly wondering what, if anything, he was going to do. Caleb simply smiled and said that it would be his signature on the forms and not the marshal's. Caleb and the marshal stared at each other for a few moments before the sheriff spoke.

'He's right, Marshal,' he said. 'It was him who brought McGovern into my office and it was him who caught Smith. Sorry, but I've got to go along with the preacher. That bounty rightly belongs to him.'

The marshal snarled and he and his men suddenly turned, kicked their horses into action and were quickly swallowed up in the darkness. Both the sheriff and the doc breathed sighs of relief.

'You're a marked man,' said the sheriff. 'There was another bounty hunter a couple of years ago who tried to claim bounty. He never showed up for his money an' we never did find out what happened to him.'

'Did Warlock claim the bounty?' asked Caleb.

'He tried to,' said the sheriff. 'Didn't get it though. The judge ruled that it was quite clear the bounty hunter was the only one legally entitled to it. But, since he never showed up, it was held by the court for six months just in case he did turn up. Never did though. After six months the money was transferred to city funds. Warlock tried claimin' it but it didn't make no difference.'

'Then I'd better make certain I put in an appearance in court,' said Caleb. 'Under the circumstances, Sheriff, I wonder if you'd mind if I spent the night in one of your cells? I would certainly feel a lot safer.'

'Don't see why not,' said the sheriff. 'Even Warlock wouldn't dare try nothin' there. Personally I don't think you're in any danger tonight wherever you stay. If nothin' else, that little episode with the other bounty hunter must've told Warlock it would have been better to have waited and let the man collect the bounty an' then take it off him.'

'Always assuming it *was* the marshal who killed him,' said Caleb. 'From what I've seen of Morgan City there must be hundreds of men of all colours who'd slit a man's throat for a dollar.'

'Yeah, hundreds,' agreed the sheriff. 'I still think it was Sam Warlock though. I might be wrong, but I don't think so. What I'm sayin' is I reckon he'll let you collect an' then kill you when you leave town. That way he settles what he thinks is a grudge and gets the money.'

'But that's against the law, it's illegal, it would be murder,' said Caleb. 'Lawmen aren't immune from the law, you should know that.'

'I know it, he knows it an' everybody else in Morgan City knows it,' agreed the sheriff. 'Only thing is, who the hell's goin' to stop him or do anythin' at all about it? That includes me. More to the point, who's goin' to prove it? As far as most folk in these parts are concerned, as a US marshal, Sam Warlock *is* the law.'

'He's right,' said the doc, who up to that point had been very quiet. 'I treated a man for serious bullet wounds once who claimed that Warlock had shot him and left him for dead for no other reason that he tried arguing with him. A complaint was made to the authorities but it came down to his word against the man he shot, so nothing was ever done. That man went out hunting one day and never returned. That might have been coincidence but it was a very odd coincidence. People tend not to argue with Sam Warlock.'

Later, in the sheriff's office and amidst a great deal of grunting on the part of the doc and cries of extreme pain on the part of Leroy Smith, the broken bones were somehow put back into a position something similar to their original and bound in splints. After that Smith became unconscious. Caleb was given a bunk in a small room off the sheriff's office and the remainder of the night passed without incident.

The first case to be brought up before Judge Hamlyn was the lawyer, James Clayton. The sheriff had warned Caleb that he might be required to testify but in the event he was not. It proved to be little more than a hearing to hold the lawyer in custody until a formal trial could begin. Caleb had already made it plain that he was prepared to forget all about the attempted murder charge and this was accepted.

It seemed that Mrs Fraser, Clayton's assistant, had been more than willing to tell all she knew about the embezzlement and her evidence was more than enough to convince the judge. James Clayton was held in jail for three months pending a thorough examination of his books. The men hired to kill Caleb were also held whilst the sheriff investigated certain other deaths related to their activities and those of the lawyer. Mrs Fraser smiled weakly at Caleb as she left the court.

There then followed a series of drunks, all of whom pleaded guilty to charges of drunkenness, disorderly conduct and breach of the peace. All six were fined five dollars and given one week to pay. Failure to pay the fine would result in a prison sentence of one month. The sheriff assured Caleb that, as local men, it was most unusual for them not to find the money, although very occasionally one would leave town without paying.

Shortly before the matter of Caleb's bounty was brought up, Marshal Sam Warlock, accompanied by one of his deputies, appeared and sat at the back of the court. Both remained completely silent as the sheriff explained to the judge what had happened and exactly who the outlaws were. Billy McGovern was briefly brought before the court simply to confirm his name.

Caleb was awarded the reward money and thanked by the judge for bringing two dangerous criminals to justice. This plainly did not go down very well with Sam Warlock, who stormed out of the court.

Caleb had expected such a large amount of cash would have to be obtained from a bank, but it appeared that Morgan City court house was large enough to have its own supply of money. Caleb was paid there and then.

There was no sign of Sam Warlock or any of his deputies as Caleb left the court but there was a man claiming to be from the local paper who wanted to run a story about Caleb. Caleb thanked him but declined to give the man any further information. This did not appear to dampen the man's enthusiasm: he already had a good headline about bounty-hunting priests, he said. Josh Brown also suddenly made an appearance.

'I heard you put one over on Sam Warlock,' said Josh. 'It's about time somebody did somethin' like that. Only hope you gets away with it, Reveren'. Word is out that the marshal is cryin' out for blood – *your* blood.'

'Word certainly travels very fast in Morgan City,' said Caleb. 'I thought he might be. If he is, he'll have to act pretty fast. I've got my money and I'm leaving Morgan City right now. Does the *word* have anything to say on what he intends doing?'

'Might do at that,' said Josh with a huge grin. 'I hear you just picked up two thousand five hundred dollars for them two outlaws. That kind of money makes the hundred dollars you gave me look like pretty small beer. Information costs money, Reveren'. I reckon I can find out what the marshal is up to, but it's goin' to cost you.'

'All in ones and fives, I suppose?' said Caleb.

Josh nodded.

'You find out what you can about Sam Warlock and meet me back here in an hour. By then I should have enough in small bills.'

'One hour!' said Josh. 'You don't give a man much time.'

'One hour,' confirmed Caleb. 'If you are not back by then or you can't find out anything, I'm leaving town no matter what.'

'OK, Reveren',' sighed Josh. 'One hour it is. How much you willin' to pay?'

'Enough to keep you in women and drink for a week or two,' said Caleb.

'Yes, sir, Reveren', sir,' grinned Josh. 'One hour it is.'

TEN

Caleb used the hour he had given Josh to collect his horse, to purchase certain essential supplies for himself and also to acquire a hundred dollars in small denomination notes. He had already decided that he was going to head west, a route which would, apparently, eventually take him through cattle country. He had no particular reason for going that way as opposed to any other route, it was simply that it was more or less the direction he had been travelling in when he had arrived in the town of Burney before his present troubles had started. He saw no reason to change his mind now.

For no other reason than curiosity and having time to waste, Caleb went to the sheriff's office and then the jail and checked on the condition of the two outlaws. Billy McGovern seemed to have completely recovered and swore at him but otherwise said nothing. Leroy Smith, now completely immobile due to his legs being strapped in large splints, did at least greet him with a weak smile and even thanked him once again for saving his life. He said that it was a pity that the only motive for doing so was money. It was plainly too soon to tell if the injuries to Smith would have any lasting or permanent effects and Caleb was not particularly interested.

The lawyer, James Clayton, warned Caleb to keep out of his way as he would eventually track him down and kill him. The men hired by Clayton refused even to look at him.

It also transpired that an official from the state capital had arrived and was at that moment examining the books and accounts of the lawyer with the full co-operation of Mrs Fraser, Clayton's assistant. The sheriff seemed to believe that she was being rather too keen to help and must therefore have something to hide. However, he was quite certain that enough proof would be forthcoming to send James Clayton to prison for a great many years. Certainly enough to make Clayton's threats against Caleb meaningless.

When he came out of the jail, Caleb was quite surprised that suddenly there seemed to be a total absence of Sam Warlock's deputies about the streets. He was not too surprised at not seeing Warlock himself, but the apparent total absence of deputies set certain alarm bells ringing in his mind. They had been present before he had gone into the jail and it seemed most strange that they should suddenly disappear.

The marshal's displeasure had hardly been hidden when the judge had awarded Caleb the bounty money and Caleb had little doubt that he was planning ways of relieving him of his new-found wealth. His concern seemed justified when Josh eventually appeared.

'Word is that Warlock is out to kill you an' take that money you got,' said Josh. 'I ain't sure just where he is right now; nobody seems to know, which ain't all that unusual. I knows for a fact though that he's got men keepin' a look out for you at every possible way out of town. I seen some of 'em myself. Yes, sir, he's got this town sewn up so tight that I don't reckon even a cock-roach could get by without bein' seen.'

'That's no more than I expected,' said Caleb. 'There's not much I can do about it either and I have to leave sometime. Anyhow, that's my problem, not yours. I've got some more money for you . . .' He handed Josh a bundle of five- and one-dollar bills. 'One hundred dollars,' he continued. 'That ought keep you happy for a couple of weeks or so. I must confess that I am rather worried about what might happen to you when I'm gone. Warlock knows who you are and that you have been helping me. For that reason alone I believe he is just as likely to kill you as he is me. Don't you think it's time you left Morgan City as well?'

'Sure, could be you is right, Reveren',' agreed Josh. 'You probably are. Only thing is, where the hell do I go? Naw, on the whole I think I'd rather take my chance with Sam Warlock right here in Morgan City. I knows almost everybody there is to know, I knows where I can get myself a bite to eat or a beer when I ain't got no money. I knows just who I can trust an' who I can't. Anyhow, I don't reckon Sam Warlock is goin' to take too much notice of me. I'm a nobody as far as he's concerned an' I sure ain't got no money, which is what he's interested in – well, I won't have once this is all gone. No, sir, leavin' Morgan City would mean me bein' out in the wide-open country an' I told you before, I ain't no country boy. I'm town-born an' bred apart from my time in the army. The bigger the town the better. All them wide-open spaces or too many trees just scare the livin' daylights out of me. It wasn't too bad when I was in the army, there was a whole crowd of us then, but I'd die out there on my own. Anyhow, I think I'd rather die of lead poisonin' from Marshal Sam Warlock's gun in this town than be killed by a bear or a pack of wolves out there an' nobody know about it.'

'I've never known wolves attack a man,' said Caleb. 'It just isn't true no matter what anyone tells you. Bears can be unpredictable sometimes and do attack for no reason but not wolves. They are nothing but stories put about by men who don't know anything about wolves.'

'I'll have take your word on that,' said Josh. 'Just don't expect me to go out there an' find out for myself if it's true or not. Which way you headed?'

'West,' said Caleb. 'I haven't the faintest idea where it leads to or what is out there, but I am sure to come across some town or other eventually. Anyway, you'd be surprised at just how much in demand a pastor or a minister of the church – any church – can be, even at the most remote of homesteads. Even a black minister is acceptable in most places. There's nearly always a christening – sometimes even of adults – and a few weddings and even the occasional funeral. Sometimes all they want is a normal church service. The more remote the homestead or small community, the more anxious they seem to be for me to perform a service or to make a relationship between man an' woman legal by getting married properly. Sometimes they get married years after they have raised a large family and might be grandparents themselves. They don't get the opportunity very often and they tend to make the most of it when they do.'

'Ain't never had no time for things like religion or gettin' wed myself,' said Josh. 'Especially gettin' wed. I had my chances but I seen too many men ruined by havin' a woman an' kids hangin' round their necks, includin' my mother. OK, Reveren', I told you all I know. It's up to you to watch out for Warlock now. I don't reckon I can help you much more. Thanks for the money, I'll make it last as long as I can. . . .' He grinned broadly. 'I guess that won't be too long though. I hope you make it but I'd say the odds were against you.'

'I've had better odds,' admitted Caleb. 'There's just one thing which puzzles me about all this. Why do you allow Sam Warlock to get away with it? It seems to me that he's nothing more than an outlaw wearing a marshal's badge.'

'An' it's that badge what makes all the difference,' said Josh. 'Sure, everybody thinks the same as you, but there just ain't nobody in Morgan City got the guts to do anythin' about it, an' that includes the sheriff. It is said that a man has to commit at least one murder before he can be considered for a job as one of Warlock's deputies. Don't know how true that is but I wouldn't be surprised. There's been a couple of folk in the past what've tried to deal with the marshal but they ended up dead. Folk just ain't prepared to die, they'd rather live with what they've got. You've gone a lot further than any other man has an' survived.'

'Why don't you all band together and do something?' asked Caleb.

'Oh, sure, don't think it hasn't been suggested,' said Josh with a dry laugh. 'There's plenty of folk what'll talk about everybody doin' somethin' an' they'll talk all day

about it, but they is the worst. They shy away from actually doin' anythin' themselves but they is only too ready
to suggest somebody else does somethin'. They'd be
the first to deny they had anythin' to do with it if it went
wrong as well. They'd also be the first to lick Warlock's
ass if he told 'em to. Still, one way or another it won't
be your problem no more, you'll either be long gone
from here or you'll be dead. If I was a bettin' man,
Reveren', I'd put every penny I've got on you bein'
dead before the day's out.'

'I thank you for that vote of confidence,' said Caleb
with a grin. 'You might well be right, but remember I
don't give in so easily.'

'Sure, I knows that,' agreed Josh. 'Only trouble is you
might have all the spunk in the world, be the fastest an'
most accurate man there ever was with a gun an' even
have right an' the law on your side, but that don't make
you invincible. It won't stop a well-aimed bullet in the
back. Not unless you know somethin' the rest of us
don't. Bullets don't care who pulls that trigger.'

Caleb laughed. It was a simple logic but a very true
one. If he was going to get away from Morgan City
unscathed he was most certainly going to need more
than spunk – as Josh had put it. He decided that the
time had come to have a word with someone in authority, somebody other than the sheriff, to try and secure a
free and safe passage out of Morgan City.

He had no doubt that the sheriff was basically a good
man but he also seemed to be a weak man. This meant
he always chose the easy option which invariably meant
going along with whatever Sam Warlock said. He
decided that the judge who had awarded him the

bounty money would be the best person to see. He appeared to have some authority and did not seem frightened of the marshal. He was in luck, he caught the judge just as he was going into his office.

Judge Hamlyn listened patiently to what Caleb had to say but was unable to offer any real solutions. He appeared to agree that Marshal Sam Warlock was indeed little more than an outlaw sponsored by the state but, as he probably rightly pointed out, until Sam Warlock was actually caught in the act of breaking the law, there was nothing anyone could do. They had tried in the past to have him removed from office but had always failed.

'How fast are you with those guns of yours?' the judge suddenly asked.

'Shall I put it this way, Your Honour,' replied Caleb. 'I don't think there are many men who are more accurate than me, but there are plenty who are whole lot faster. Why do you ask?'

'The thought crossed my mind,' said the judge, 'that if you were engaged in a fair fight with Marshal Warlock and he just happened to be killed, it would solve everyone's problems.'

Caleb laughed. 'And just how does anyone pick a *fair* fight with a United States marshal?'

'Yes indeed, how?' agreed the judge. 'I was simply thinking out loud, that's all. Take no notice of me.'

'Surely something can be done to prevent him blocking my way out of town, following me, stealing my money and probably murdering me? I want something done about it *before* somebody discovers my body.'

'Proof, Reverend,' said the judge. 'Do you have

proof that that is his intention? Proof which would stand up in court, real proof? I don't think you do. The word of your friend Josh Brown would hardly qualify as proof of any kind especially as it would appear the man has been in your pay. If you have no proof then everything is simply a matter of your word against that of the marshal. The word of a minister of the church who just happens to be a bounty hunter against the word of an upholder of the law. With all respect to your calling as a minister, which might hold some sway on its own, there would be no contest in any court of law between the word of a bounty hunter, even though he is a minister or pastor, and that of a United States marshal.'

'So there's nothing you can do except wait for my body to turn up?' said Caleb. 'I don't much care for that idea.'

'That is not quite what I said,' said the judge. 'I would say that every man worth his salt in Morgan City would agree that you should be allowed to carry on with your legal business without fear or prejudice. Should it ever come to the point of charging Marshal Warlock with your murder I would relish the prospect of his being in my court.'

'I hope you don't mind if I do not share your enthusiasm,' said Caleb. 'You said something about a fair fight. If and only if, I should agree to such a hare-brained idea and I did happen to kill him, who would decide if it was a fair fight or not? What guarantee would I have that I would not be charged with his murder just to make it look right to those in higher authority?'

'Ah,' sighed the judge, 'there you have another difficulty. The only thing I can say is that there would not be too many people who would be pushing for your conviction, not even in higher authority, as you put it.'

'In other words you want to hire me to kill him,' said Caleb. 'As you yourself have noted, I am a minister of the church and as such I cannot agree to assassinating anyone. I am not now and never have been a hired killer.'

'Assassination, hire, Reverend?' said the judge with a laugh. 'I would be the last person in the world to suggest such a thing. I am merely pointing out that there would be very few, if any, who would claim that you deliberately killed the marshal. Without witnesses or proper proof, you could never be charged. The same thing could be said if the marshal's body were to be found somewhere.'

Caleb laughed. 'In the words of my friend Josh,' he said, 'I'll just have to take your word on that. Just don't expect me to go out there and find out if it's true or not. I am asking you for an escort out of the city for as far as it takes for me to feel safe. I'm sure you can order the sheriff to provide me with such an escort.'

'Order?' queried the judge. 'I think you have the wrong idea of my authority. I can order all sorts of things in my court but I cannot make orders of that sort.' The judge hunched forward and looked Caleb squarely in the eyes. 'I shall now be perfectly honest with you, Reverend. I awarded you that bounty because you were quite legally entitled to it and I had no alternative. I also knew very well exactly what the marshal's reaction would be. I knew that he would want to kill you and steal that money.'

153

'You mean you deliberately tried to provoke this fight between us?' snapped Caleb. 'You were hoping that I would kill Warlock and so get rid of your problem. You were hoping to use me!'

'I regret to say you are quite right,' replied the judge. 'It would also appear that I have succeeded. I believe it is now simply a matter of time before either yourself or the marshal is killed by the other one. However, I think you must agree that in many ways you have brought it upon yourself; it needed very little prompting from the likes of me. From what I have heard, it would appear that you were quite determined that Marshal Sam Warlock would *not* collect that bounty. I believe that something of a feud developed between the two of you.'

'I was legally entitled, as you pointed out,' said Caleb. 'You could be right though. OK, Your Honour.' Caleb gave a deep sigh and anger began to well up inside him which he tried to quell. In some ways the truth hurt. 'That much I accept, but your problems with Warlock are all of your own making and happened long before I appeared. It looks like Josh was right. Everybody talks but nobody does anything and expects somebody else to do their dirty work. So it's no thanks to you I might be dead the moment I walk out of this door. Sorry to waste your time, *Your Honour.* One way or another this is probably the last time you will ever see me – at least alive. I can't hang about Morgan City for the remainder of my life, what might be left of it.'

Judge Hamlyn smiled weakly as Caleb left his office. Outside, he thought he saw Josh hurrying away from the sheriff's office, but he could not be certain. Caleb decided to go into the office, where he told the sheriff what he had told the judge and what he had been told. The sheriff nodded sagely but told Caleb there was nothing he could do, which was exactly what he had expected. So far Marshal Sam Warlock had not broken any laws. At least there was absolutely no proof of any crime. The sheriff needed much more than common talk before he could act.

'Spineless, everybody in Morgan City is spineless,' declared Caleb, now feeling more anger than he had felt for a long time At the same time he knew in his heart that it was anger brought on by the fact that his own stubbornness meant that *he* was now the main loser. 'I don't swear very often, it never achieves anything, but right now I feel like yelling and swearing at every man in this god-forsaken place. One way or another I've put my life on the line but every damned one of you is shit scared of Sam Warlock and I have to ask why. Perhaps it is just his name. A warlock is a male witch, a magician. Well, there's no doubt he has certainly lived up to his name so far. He's used his magic to scare you all, to control you, to make you all do exactly what he tells you to do. What's wrong with everybody? He's just another man. His shit stinks just the same as yours and when he's cut he bleeds red blood exactly the same as anyone else.'

'Call us what you will, Reverend,' said the sheriff. 'So far you haven't said a thing what ain't true, I know that. I agree with everythin' you say but I'm sorry to say it simply ain't goin' to make a scrap of difference. Nobody, includin' Judge Hamlyn, ain't goin' to do nothin' at all. You're on your own.'

Caleb stormed out of the office. It was very rare for

him to feel as angry as he did at that moment. His thoughts as to what he wished might happen to various people were far from Christian and he spent at least ten minutes recovering his composure. His mood was not helped in that Judge Hamlyn was quite right, there had been something of a feud between himself and Warlock and he had, in many ways, brought it upon himself. Eventually he mounted his horse and cast one last jaundiced eye around. This was most definitely one town he intended never to come to again should he be fortunate enough to survive.

He saw the sheriff come out of his office to stand on the boardwalk and to watch him ride away and he thought he saw Judge Hamlyn looking out of his office window, but he could not be certain. There was only one face he would not have minded seeing again, but there was no sign of Josh Brown. He had apparently wisely made himself scarce.

For the first time since leaving the jail that morning, Caleb came across two of the marshal's deputies. They made no attempt to stop him or to go for their guns but Caleb could not resist the temptation to shout at them and tell them to run to their employer and inform him that he was leaving town. Neither of them said a thing but one of them *did* run off down a side-street. The other found his horse and proceeded to follow him. By the time Caleb had reached the edge of Morgan City, he realized that he had at least ten deputies following him.

Caleb might have been very accurate with a gun, but even he knew that such odds were completely impossible to overcome. He rode on, the deputies still following but making no attempt to catch up with him. It appeared that they wanted him clear of the city limits before they acted. There was no sign of Marshal Sam Warlock.

They passed the last building and were crossing farmland but still the deputies remained some fifty yards behind. Nor did they make any attempt to catch up with him once the farmland had been crossed some twenty minutes later.

Caleb guessed that the fact they had passed several homesteads and farms had a great deal to do with the absence of action. There were plainly too many potential witnesses, but why they still remained behind when there were no more farms he did not know. All he could do was to ride on and hope that they were doing nothing more than escorting him out of Morgan City.

The trail eventually led along a narrow valley between two quite steep hills, which at some points was no more than twenty or thirty feet in width. The sides of the hills were quite thickly wooded but far too steep to be easily climbed by a horse. The deputies remained where they were, which on this occasion was understandable. It would have been impossible even for ten of them to get the better of Caleb in such a confined space. However, Caleb did draw his two Colts, tucked one in his belt and the other he rested between his legs on his saddle.

Quite suddenly the trail opened out into a basin about sixty or seventy yards across. There was a small waterfall, about thirty feet high, on the right-hand edge. The small stream ran across the basin and disappeared between two tall rocks, the gap between them no more than four feet. On the far side the trail ascended the side of the basin and disappeared over the rim and amongst some trees.

Marshal Sam Warlock suddenly stepped from behind one of the very few trees in the basin, his rifle casually slung in the crook of his arm.

'This is about as far as you go I reckon, Reverend,' said Warlock. 'I told you nobody don't collect no bounty for nobody in my territory. You should've listened to what I said. That way you might've been ridin' through here a free man now. As it is, you are about to die. Still, you're a religious man – at least you claim to be – so you won't mind too much about dyin'. Preachers is always goin' on about heaven. Now's your chance to find out if it's really there or not.'

'On the contrary, I object to dying most strongly,' said Caleb, raising the gun on the saddle. 'You first or me?' he invited.

Sam Warlock simply laughed. 'Right now there's ten guns aimed at you, Reverend. They're all about five yards away from your back. I must be a good thirty yards from you and one thing I've learned in my time is that the chances of you even hittin' me from that distance with even the best pistol are somethin' like a hundred to one against. Even if you did hit me it's probably another five hundred to one against you killing me. Go ahead, Reverend, shoot, I've been shot before. You shoot first an' I get the perfect alibi. I was actin' in self-defence.'

'Since it would seem that it is your intention to kill me,' said Caleb, 'I really don't see that it makes any difference.'

'But it'd make all the difference as far as I'm concerned,' a voice suddenly boomed out from somewhere behind Caleb. A look of alarm spread across Sam Warlock's face and Caleb turned to look behind.

He could hardly believe his eyes at the sight which greeted him. The sheriff, three deputies and at least ten other men had more or less surrounded Warlock's deputies. The biggest surprise of all was the fact that Josh Brown was amongst them, carrying a rifle and even seemed to be one of the leaders. All except the sheriff had their guns trained on the deputies.

'Drop your guns,' the sheriff ordered the deputies. 'Any man who doesn't do so gets himself shot.' Reluctantly all the deputies dropped their guns. 'You too, Marshal,' instructed the sheriff.

'You are exceeding your authority, Sheriff,' said Warlock. 'Your authority ends at the city limits. This is my territory. Not only are you exceeding your authority but I shall see to it that you are replaced as sheriff. Everybody knows you've been trying to get rid of me for years. I think you want my job. Sorry, Sheriff, it just ain't goin' to work. I have too much influence in high places.'

'Judge Hamlyn extended my authority,' said the sheriff. 'I think there are more than enough witnesses to what you said to ensure that it is you who are removed from office, not me.'

'Got it all worked out, haven't you,' grated Warlock. 'I could still kill that damned preacher an' get away with it quite easily.' He almost casually raised his rifle and aimed it at Caleb. . . .

It was a single shot but it hit the marshal straight

between the eyes. Josh Brown slowly lowered his rifle and smiled at Caleb.

'I was the best shot in my regiment,' he said. 'I won many a bet shootin' bugs off walls an' trees. Sorry, Sheriff,' he continued. 'I thought he might just be stupid enough to kill the lieutenant. You can charge me with murder if you want.'

'I don't think that will be necessary,' said the sheriff. 'I'm also quite certain he did intend to shoot.'

'Thanks, Josh,' said Caleb. 'I guess I owe you. What are you going to do now?'

'Much the same as usual,' said Josh. 'Just pray for me sometimes. I ain't never had nobody pray for me before. Now get goin' before I starts gettin' all weepy.'

'Was he right about you wanting his job?' Caleb asked the sheriff.

'Let's put it this way, Reveren'. If they ask me I won't refuse. Now, do as the man says, get the hell out of here. In the meantime I need another deputy. Your friend Josh seems ideal. He knows everybody there is to know. He's a good shot and as far as I know he's never done anythin' wrong. At least not in Morgan City.'

'There was fifty dollars out on me a few years ago,' said Josh. 'I robbed a grocery store on account of I was hungry just after I was released from the army.'

'You and hundreds of others,' said the sheriff. 'I think we can forget about that. Now get goin' Reveren'.'

Caleb laughed and got going.